DUMB MOVE

SEI ASSASSIN THRILLER #6

TY HUTCHINSON

1

We called them scavies. They were the opportunists who jumped on open contracts. They weren't assassins by trade—leeches would best describe them. And I had a dozen or so of those bloodsuckers trying their best to take me down.

I had my back pressed against the wall in the hallway near the top of a stairwell. Lying a few feet away from me were five dead men from a local Latino gang: Norteños. Pounding footsteps were making their way up the stairs. I drew a deep breath as I gripped my Glock tighter.

Five steps away.

Wait, Sei.

Four steps.

Wait.

Three.

Now!

I raised my handgun and fired into the temple of the first gang member to enter the hallway. I dropped to a squat and shot the knee of the second man to come off the stairs. He crumpled to the floor, howling, and I fired two more bullets into his face to shut him up. I ejected my spent magazine and loaded a fresh one. I'd heard enough pounding on the stairs to know there were three of them coming up. The third one was still on the stairs.

I moved forward, gun out front until I reached the corner. His heavy breaths told me he was either on the second or third stair from the top. I stuck my gun around the corner and fired twice. I heard a moan and then the sound of him tumbling down the stairs.

The thing about scavies was they weren't really that much of a threat. They were unskilled, unorganized, and unbelievably stupid. But what they lacked in skill, they made up for in numbers. My wasting time and energy dealing with them would give a professional—a trained assassin—an advantage when striking. I was alone, with no one to watch my back. And that was the entire point of the open contract.

The man who put the contract on my head was an ex: Ethan Carmotte, a vengeful man I had left eighteen years ago. He knew me well enough to know that sending hitman after hitman for me was futile. I would dispatch them as they came. But with an open contract and an obnoxious payout—$50 million—it would be impossible for me to see every attack coming. I still liked to think I could.

Why the contract?

Ethan is the biological father of my daughter. When he found out about her, he wanted her, but not for the reasons you would think. He wanted to punish me. Taking her away from me would do just that. He was still bitter about my leaving him. He was a maniac. The last thing I had wanted was to subject my unborn child to a man like him. The second I discovered I was pregnant, I made the decision to leave him.

My daughter's name is Mui. For seventeen years, Ethan had no clue she existed. And then one day he learned the truth and managed to kidnap her. I had no choice but to come for her.

Long story short, I got her back—but now that he knew we were both alive, he'd never stop coming for us. So I put my daughter into hiding and made myself the sole target: hence, the contract.

But back to the scavies.

I had needed weapons and ammunition quick. I had a contact in the Mission, a neighborhood in San Francisco known for Latino gang activity. My contact wasn't associated with any of the gangs, but I had wrongly assumed I could trust him. Why? I'd known him for twenty years. I realized a $50 million payout would have people flipping on me. I just didn't expect him to be one of them. From that point forward, I'd have to rethink every friendly before contacting them for help.

Armando Lopez was the arms dealer I'd gone to see. He lived on the top floor of an apartment complex in the middle of Norteños territory. While Lopez wasn't strictly affiliated with the gang, he supplied them.

Everything seemed fine when I met with Lopez. I gave him my order beforehand. He had the supplies ready when I arrived: handguns, a mini assault rifle, suppressors, knives, and ammunition. I transferred the money to his offshore account, grabbed my gear, and exited his apartment, only to face a hallway full of Norteños.

They stood casually, hands buried deep inside their saggy jeans with smug looks plastered across their faces. They assumed this tiny woman was easy money. Wrong. I used a single knife to carve my way past them. I didn't even have to drop the duffel bag I carried in my other hand. Amateurs.

I traded the knife for the Glock I'd bought from Lopez. I had places to be and didn't have time to waste. I'd received a tip that Ethan was in San Francisco. If you're wondering how reliable the information was, it came from Ethan himself. It was one of the many games that man loved to play. What he really wanted was a front-row seat to what he thought would be my demise.

Cut back to me getting out of that apartment building.

Down the stairs I went while peering over the railing. Two more gang members were making their way up. One fired a shotgun at me. I pulled back in time to avoid being shot in the face. I fired through the railings, striking the shooter in the center of his forehead. My second shot hit his partner behind him in the cheek. I fired again, ending him. I was on the landing between the sixth and fifth floors. I still had a ways to go.

A grenade bounced off a wall near me and settled on the stairs to reach the fifth-floor hallway. I bolted down the hall, avoiding the shrapnel from the blast. But as luck would have it, the hallway ended with a brick wall, and every apartment door I passed was closed.

Norteños were running after me. I fired twice, hitting one and backing the rest of the group off, but seconds later, they returned fire. Finally, an apartment door opened, and a confused man poked his head out. I slipped right inside.

"I apologize," I said as I ran past him toward the balcony.

I slipped the duffel bag over my shoulder, hopped the balcony railing, and hung with just one hand. I swung my legs and landed on the balcony below. Into the apartment I went, past a startled family. I apologized again and headed straight to the front door. I burst out into the fourth-floor hallway only to see about twenty gang members running down the hall toward me.

I ran back into the apartment and out to the balcony. I hopped over the railing and hung by one hand, repeating the swinging motion to the patio below me. But by then, the gang members had smartened up and appeared on other balconies and fired at me.

There wasn't much cover on the balcony. I had little choice

2

During an earlier phone conversation with Ethan, he said something very telling: "I can see it all from the eye in the sky." One place in San Francisco came to mind: the Transamerica Pyramid. The triangle-shaped building, a staple of the city skyline, had a light at the very tiptop that lit up at night: the Crown Jewel, as locals referred to it.

If I had to name a fault of Ethan's, it would be his mouth. He often said more than necessary.

You might think Ethan would be an easy target for me. He isn't. He's trained equally well. Perhaps the only person I'd ever met that gave me pause, he had all the required skills of an assassin and the mindset of a psychopath. Ethan was extremely dangerous. Couple that with his immense wealth, and there wasn't much out of his reach.

While I dated him, I learned very little about what he actually did to generate that money. But one thing was clear to me: the sway he held over influential people in the world—prime ministers, presidents, warlords, military generals, businessmen —they were all afraid of him. And rarely did someone cross him. But when they did, Ethan always made an example of them that made others shudder.

I never understood how he had developed and maintained those relationships, but that was how he manifested his power. However, it must be said, those people weren't exactly angels. They were as corrupt as they came and also got something out of the relationship. But make no mistake, Ethan called the shots. The cabal that everyone likes to talk about as secretly controlling the world? There is no such group. It's Ethan Carmotte.

For decades, Ethan had been able to keep his true identity hidden, speaking only through trusted men. Rarely did he meet people in person. In fact, everyone knew him as Arthur. He once told me he likened himself to King Arthur, and the people who obeyed him were the knights of his round table. But not long ago, I exposed his true identity—the first chink in his armor. And believe me, I intended on breaking down his defenses until I destroyed him.

And it wasn't because he put a contract on my head, though that certainly didn't help.

It was what he did to his own flesh and blood, his daughter. After kidnapping her, he used her as bait and waited for me to strike. Given the opportunity, he'd do it again. Mui was nothing to him but a means to get to me, the true prize. Until Ethan was dead, Mui and I would always be looking over our shoulders.

I gave the bike a bit more gas and sped in between cars along Market Street toward the Transamerica building. I figured he was on the top floor, and I didn't exactly have a plan for how I would gain access undetected. The building itself was off-limits to the public. Only employees of the companies housed in the building and their guests were allowed passage past the lobby.

When I got there, I headed into the narrow park that ran between the Transamerica building and a parking lot. I kept my helmet on and found a bench away from people. I slipped off my small backpack and quickly took stock of my supplies: One handgun with eight bullets in the magazine. Of the magazines I had scavenged, two were fully loaded; one held half the amount and the other about a quarter. I figured I had less than fifty rounds.

Credentials aside, I wasn't exactly dressed like an office employee or someone arriving for a meeting. I had on a black leather jacket, blue jeans, and steel-toed boots. Even if I could get by security in the lobby, I assumed a keycard might be needed to use the elevator.

Part of me thought to throw discretion to the side and bull-doze my way in. Take the security guard with me and force him to take me to the top floor. I'd have about ten, maybe fifteen minutes at the most, to find Ethan, dispatch him, and leave before law enforcement showed. That was if my assumption about him being there in the first place was correct. Just then, my cell phone rang.

"Where are you, darling?"

It was Ethan.

"I heard you had problems when you paid Lopez a visit. Honestly, I'm surprised you went to him. His supply is bottom of the barrel. Nothing he has is worthy of you or of high caliber. But then again, I suppose you felt you just needed some weapons really quick. Have you figured out where I am?"

I had no interest in answering him. That's what he really wanted—a response, a chance to rile me up.

"You're outside. I can hear the automobile traffic in the distance. I know you're listening to me, Sei. I hear your breath. Either you're getting old, or you're getting rusty. Probably both. Well, I thought I'd check in, as I am getting bored sitting here waiting for someone skilled to come after you. I hear people all over the world are eager to take a chance on the contract. Some of your old pals have even come out of retirement. Can you

But I was within reach of Ethan. I couldn't squander the opportunity. If it meant attacking the Hop Sing Boys and starting a war with their leadership back in Hong Kong, the Wo Hop To, so be it.

I removed my helmet and placed it back on the bike seat. "I expect this to be here when I return," I said to the men.

I kept my handgun pressed against my thigh as I walked. The entrance to the tong was a single glass door with a dark tint. Why the lack of security? The Hop Sing Boys controlled Chinatown. The minute anyone entered Waverly, they were aware of it.

I reached for the door, and it was pulled open before I could push it. Standing in the doorway was a young man. If he was armed with a weapon, it was still tucked into the waistband of his jeans.

"I'm looking for Ethan Carmotte."

The man said nothing, his face expressionless. I raised my handgun, pressed the barrel against his forehead, and backed him up the stairs until we reached the second floor. There were two more Triads there. Both were armed with shorty shotguns.

The Hop Sing Boys had installed a new enforcer a few years ago. I knew of him but had never met him personally. His name was Fan Sung. I couldn't be sure what orders he had given his men, but it was strange that nothing was being said, and I was allowed to walk in with my weapon pressed against the head of one of their own. The young man standing in front of me smirked as he chuckled.

I reacted by firing once into his head. Three Triads burst through the entrance and made their way up the stairs. I fired three times, cutting them down. The two holding the shorty shotguns opened fire, shattering parts of the balustrade.

A stinging pain ripped through my left arm as I ducked. A sizeable wooden splinter had punctured the top of my hand. I yanked it out quickly. The men continued to fire, and their footsteps told me they were advancing. I managed to shoot one in his knee and then again in his neck. The remaining man aimed his shotgun over the railing and fired blindly. I grabbed an assault rifle off of a dead Triad on the stairs. With my cheek pressed against the stock, I looked down the iron sights and hurried up the stairs.

Click!

Click!

He was reloading.

I popped up onto the second floor, tapping the trigger three times. He went down, and I hurried to the stairs leading up to the third floor. I peered around the corner and fired at the man waiting at the top, backing him off. I had already made up my mind I was eliminating everyone in that building, including Sung.

Before I reached the top stair, I crouched. Gunfire erupted, making Swiss cheese of the balustrade. I traded fire with the Triads who were raining bullets down on my location.

This is taking too long.

I dove onto the landing and slid across the polished wooden floor while firing at the legs of the three Triads. They all dropped, and I tapped bullets into the tops of their heads. There was one more floor plus a small room at the very top. I knew that because I had once stayed at the tong long ago, under the old leadership.

I hurried up the next set of stairs. That floor was darker than the others, and I slowed my steps.

"Sei!" A voice called out. It wasn't Ethan's.

Looking through the iron sights of the assault rifle, I peered through the balusters. Sitting at a large, round table was a man dressed in a black Mao suit. I assumed it was Sung. He was unarmed and didn't look happy to see me.

Candles and a few table lamps provided the light. All of the man. He had retired a long time ago. But the bounty on my head was too high to ignore.

A split second later, he sprung to life, by removing his hat. With the flick of his wrist, blades appeared around the edges of the brim. The hat left his fingers, flying across the street like a Frisbee. I barely had enough time to move my head out of the way as the whoosh of the flying hat passed by my face.

Someone in the crowd yelled out. The hat had lodged itself into the face of the old man who had been smiling. Red streaks streamed down his cheeks. An instant later, he collapsed. I looked back at the Fisherman, but he'd disappeared. I spun in a circle, searching the now-panicked crowd, and found him on the sidewalk behind me.

Another quick flick of his wrist and a chain whip unraveled, about nine feet long. It looked and acted like a whip, but one that was made out of jointed steel pieces with a hooked blade at the end. The Fisherman twirled the whip around his head and then in a downward crisscross motion.

As he quickly advanced toward me, the whip whistled as it cut through the air. The whip moved too fast for the eye to see. I'd have to watch his arm movements to determine where it would strike next.

I backed off, keeping my distance from the deadly blade at the end. He cast the whip at me, and I narrowly avoided it. The blade at the end struck the sidewalk with a loud clank, chipping the concrete.

He yanked it back and wound up once more, casting it horizontally. I ran toward the building, leaped up, and kicked off into a backward somersault to avoid the hook. I landed on my feet and shot forward before he could swing the whip back. Distance was the hole in his defense. So long as I stayed close to him, I was in no danger of being hooked.

I struck quickly with my palm to his face, knocking him back on his feet while my other hand gripped the whip to gain control. I yanked down, trying to force it from his grip, but he held steady. The Fisherman snapped tight kicks to the outside of my thigh in quick succession. I yanked hard again on the whip, bringing him closer to me, and delivered multiple fist strikes.

He yanked back on the whip with both hands, I felt it slip from my grip, and I let go just in time to prevent the blade at the end from slicing my hand in half. I jumped up and kicked the bottom of his jaw with my boot, snapping his head up. A high kick to the side of his face knocked a tooth out of his mouth.

The Fisherman backed off before I could strike again. Blood poured from his mouth. A quick flick of his wrist and the whip wrapped around my arm quickly, leaving me no time to react as it tightened and the hook at the end cut into my left forearm. The sleeve of my leather jacket kept the hook from cutting deeper, but it was temporary. His next move would be to yank and lodge the hook into my arm. I pulled forward and down on the whip. He was taller than me but skinny, and he flew easily toward me. I cocked my head back and timed it so my forehead slammed into his nose.

The Fisherman let out a cry.

I unhooked the blade from my arm and then passed it across his neck, opening up his carotid artery. The Fisherman let out a gargling cry as his hands shot up to his neck to stem the blood flow. I unwrapped the whip from my forearm and stabbed the blade into his left eye. I backed away as he dropped to one knee. The life continued to drain from his wound, and I had no desire to stick around for the end.

It had begun. The contract was in play, and I could expect attacks at any moment. I hurried back to my motorcycle and sped away from Chinatown toward the Golden Gate Bridge to begin my cross-country journey. New York was my destination.

description of me. She could also describe my bike and provide my most recent location. If those details were to be added to the dossier, my hunt for Ethan would become that much harder. I fired a single bullet into her forehead.

I climbed into the van and searched the driver. We had identical handguns, so I took his ammunition. I had no use for the assault rifle the other man had been wielding. Riding a motorcycle with that would only draw attention.

I headed inside the small convenience store where the station attendant would be. No surprise, the place was empty. I found the recording device for the shop's security camera and shoved it into the small backpack I wore. I headed back to my motorcycle, where I discovered the engine had taken a couple of bullets. I climbed onto the bike, and to my surprise, it started. The motor didn't quite hum like it had previously. There was a chance I'd break down in the middle of nowhere, or worse, in a town where my location would be added to the dossier. But I had no choice but to carry on through the night.

The Walker River Paiute Reservation, home of the Walker River Paiute Tribe, is located southeast of Reno. The reservation is small, quiet, and full of good-natured people, except for one individual: Iron Wolf. Iron Wolf wasn't a member of the Paiute Tribe, but nobody had questioned her arrival a few days ago.

No one believed Iron Wolf was a woman until they saw her. Her fierce reputation certainly didn't match the big brown eyes used to stare down her targets. It was often repeated that Iron Wolf loved to rip the throats out of her victims.

Iron Wolf wasn't there to play house with the woman she settled with. She was after Sei. The open contract had brought her north to Nevada from Texas. Sei had been reported to be in San Francisco, with sightings of her heading east. Iron Wolf intended to track her down and kill her. And if anyone was capable of finding her, it was Iron Wolf.

Iron Wolf's father was a member of a legendary tactical unit employed by Immigration and Customs Enforcement known as the Shadow Wolves. The unit was composed solely of Native American trackers. They were responsible for tracking and taking down smugglers along the U.S.–Mexico border. When the surveillance equipment used by Border Patrol failed, the trackers excelled.

From a young age, Iron Wolf's father taught her how to track animals and people across any type of terrain. It was unusual for a girl to want to develop these skills. Still, she was a natural at it, and her father realized the potential early on. He groomed her, hopeful that she would follow in his footsteps and join the pres tigious unit one day. That never happened.

A disgruntled Border Patrol agent leaked her father's identity to the Sinaloa Cartel. Sicarios had been dispatched, and her father was later found gutted and hanging from a highway overpass. The U.S. government never acknowledged the death, nor did they even thank her family for her father's service. That never sat right with Iron Wolf, and her rage took over.

Iron Wolf figured if Sei was heading east, she'd move along Interstate 80. This continuous stretch of the highway started in San Francisco and ended in New Jersey. Iron Wolf wasn't sure where Sei was heading. She didn't care.

Iron Wolf sat shirtless at a small desk while looking at a tablet. She raised both arms above her head and stretched before knotting her long black hair into a ponytail. A large tattoo of a wolf covered her back. She adjusted the small desk lamp, the only source of light in the dark bedroom. Behind her, a woman lay sleeping in the bed.

Iron Wolf was busy studying the I-80 route to determine how much ground Sei could have made since she was thought to have left San Francisco. Of course, there were reports that she might have headed south toward Los Angeles. Still, Iron Wolf believed Sei's best shot at staying out of sight was to head toward the Great Plains. These extensive flatlands extended east of the Rocky Mountains to the Mississippi River. California had too many assassins interested in the contract, not to mention a high number of scavies wanting in on the action. Chatter on the message boards was intense, as this was the contract of a lifetime.

She assumed Sei would travel at night while lying low during the day. Sei couldn't be that far east of the reservation. Iron Wolf had no restrictions on travel. She'd catch up to Sei soon enough.

Iron Wolf had already officially registered her participation. Rarely did a contract require this, but considering the amount of the bounty, it was necessary. Anyone who successfully killed Sei but did not register would not be paid. Also, registering gave Iron Wolf access to Sei's dossier and any updated reports of her location.

There were two pieces of evidence required to claim the bounty:

- Death by any means.
- Clear photos of Sei's body and face.

Fail to meet either of those requirements, and payment would not be made. Also, anyone currently under investigation by law enforcement or captured by law enforcement after killing Sei would not be paid. Those last two rules were put in place to discourage scavies.

Iron Wolf turned off the tablet and shoved it into a backpack filled with other essential gear. She slipped a tight T-shirt over her fit torso before putting on a leather jacket and grabbing her helmet. She hopped on her black Honda Rebel. Attached to the left side of the bike was a leather holster where she kept a sawed-off shotgun. It wasn't often she had a chance to use the weapon while riding. Iron Wolf hoped Sei would give her the opportunity.

they understood the implications. Sadly, the man who stared too long did not.

Don't ask me why I dated Ethan. I was young and stupid at the time. It's a mistake that has haunted me ever since. Upon finding out I was with child, I immediately left him and went underground. I had kept my daughter's existence, even her birth, a secret from everyone. Alas, he discovered who she was in the way I feared most. Mui's curiosity about her father had pushed her to seek him out, and in doing so, she revealed her identity to the devil himself.

In the back of my mind, I'd always known I'd have to face Ethan again. It was unavoidable. I couldn't stay hidden and keep Mui a secret for the rest of our lives.

On my journey east, I had considered stopping in Reno, but Willie's words echoed through my head: "Get here fast, Sei." Traveling at night was the best way to stay out of sight. The bike also seemed to be running reasonably well despite being shot up.

I avoided driving straight through Reno and took highways that led around it. Once clear of "the biggest little city in the world," I merged back onto I-80 and settled in for a quiet drive in the night.

That lasted three hours before the engine sputtered and conked out. I coasted over to the shoulder of the highway and tried my best to restart the bike. The fuel gauge told me I had more than half a tank left. It had to be the damage from the bullet strikes.

The next town was Carlin, and it was a forty-minute walk from where I was. There was nothing but public wildland all around me, so I had no choice but to walk toward that town. The upside was that the moon was nearly full.

Not far from the side of the highway, lay train tracks

belonging to Union Pacific Railroad. According to the map on my phone, the tracks ran alongside I-80. Following them seemed like a better idea than walking on the side of the highway. I pushed the bike off the shoulder and into the brush. I did my best to conceal it with a bunch of branches. I didn't need my helmet, so I ditched that for the ball cap I carried in my backpack.

When I reached Carlin, it looked dead, really more like a rest stop. There would be no hope of finding alternative transport, so I continued on. There was a much larger town up ahead: Spring Creek.

The train tracks veered away from the highway and further into the public lands on the way there. Even though the highway was no longer visible, I stayed the course, as I knew the train tracks would eventually lead me straight to Spring Creek.

Lost in my own thoughts, it took longer for me to pick up on movement to my right. I stopped and drew my handgun while I scanned the area. A beat later, I spotted a moving shadow, and it wasn't a coyote. I took aim.

The crack of a branch sounded behind me, and I quickly glanced over my shoulder. Another shadowy figure had appeared, about thirty yards away. Within a minute, ten more figures had come out of hiding and circled around me.

I studied them for a moment. Judging from the clothing, they appeared to be vagrants. I realized then what territory I had stumbled into. These men were members of a gang known as Hobo Nation.

"Nah, we're heading to Britt, Iowa." He pointed to a shack. "That's where Junks is. Wait outside. I need to announce you."

I stood a few feet away from the shack, surrounded by the men who had escorted me. A few minutes later, and Junks stood in the doorway.

"Sei," he said in a commanding baritone voice. A smile graced his face. "It's been ages." He placed a hand on my shoulder and gave a gentle squeeze. "Come inside. You must be hungry."

The inside of the shack was surprisingly large and nicer than what I had expected based on the outside. There was a small bed, a sofa, and a couple of chairs. A couple of kerosene lamps kept the place lit, and a piece of tarp covered the ground. In the corner was a small brick stove with a chimney leading up and out of the shack. It radiated warmth.

"Take a seat," Junks said as he pointed to the sofa. I slipped my backpack off and sat.

When straightened up, Junks stood close to six feet five inches. He had a bulky chest and long dreadlocks that reminded me of the creature from the Predator movies. He made me feel even shorter than I was.

My eyes continued to study the dwelling. A covered pot was on the stove. Junks scooped food from it into a bowl and then handed it to me along with a spoon.

"Have you ever tried hobo stew?"

"I don't believe I have."

"First time for everything. Eat up. It's warm and filling."

Junks sat across from me and leaned forward, resting his forearms on top of his thighs. He took a deep breath. His back rose in the process.

"I would ask what brings you here, but I already know. V are you going to do, Sei? You can't run forever."

"I have no intention to run, nor will I hide."

"You plan on taking Carmotte down?"

"I do."

"It'll be hard with the number of people gunning for you. You're safe here, under my watch. I'll give you that peace of mind."

"I need safe passage. As far as you can take me."

"I'm traveling as far as Britt, Iowa. I can vouch for the group who will accompany me, but I cannot promise that hobos outside of this jungle won't come for you."

"That's all I'm asking."

"I'll remind you that anything east of the Mississippi River I have no control over. I only oversee the tracks belonging to Union Pacific. The railroads in the east are dangerous, Sei. I recommend you find an alternative form of travel. I also recommend you avoid the steel corridor. That's any part of I-80 running through Indiana."

"Why is that?"

"That's Steelie territory. They're just a gang, but they have numbers. If they decide to jump on your contract, they have the men to bog you down and even take your head. Are you friendly with any of the Indian reservations? There are many of them spread out across the plains."

"Not in particular. Why?"

"Just trying to gauge how screwed you are."

"I appreciate your comforting words."

"Sei, your biggest pain in the ass will be the scavies. They'll be a distraction. With no one watching your back, it'll make it easier for a professional to come up on you."

"I'm aware of the danger. Do you have weapons?" I asked.

"You know how we operate. No handguns or rifles." Junks up and removed an item from a nearby chest.

made this one myself," he said as he held up a flail. "The is made out of solid oak. It's strong. The chain is an old dog collar. The sphere is solid steel with spikes welded onto it." He swung it around. "It'll crack a skull right open."

"Give me something I can throw," I said.

"Knives." He reached back into the chest. "I cut these from a metal sheet and sharpened them. These are just as good as any fancy titanium throwing knives... I'm surprised you haven't already geared up."

"I tried to back in San Francisco, but my contact turned on me."

Junks let out a large breath as he shook his head. "Well, you can always get what you need in Chicago, but it's risky, and the people there might also pull the same bullshit as your guy in San Francisco. Is there anyone else you can turn to, someone small and under the radar?"

"There is, but it's been a while since I've reached out to that person."

Junks retook his seat and motioned for me to eat my stew. I took a bite. It was a cross between beef stew and chili.

"It's good, right? Your man Junks can cook." His toothy smile appeared on his face.

"Yes, it's good."

"The fella that brought you here, I trust him with my life. You can, too."

"What's his name?"

"We call him Cagey Mike. When I first met him eight years ago, that guy was jumpier than a frog. Always looking over his shoulder. Never trusted anyone until he met me."

"And now?"

"Still jumpy, but trustworthy."

"You never asked where I was heading," I said.

"That's because I don't want to know. The less anybody knows about your plans, the better off you are. And that includes me."

The black motor home looked more like a speeding bullet on the highway than the classic motor home associated with retirees cruising around the country. This one was matte black with graphite accents. A dark tint covered all of the windows. It resembled a tour bus more than it did an RV. On the roof of the vehicle were two mini helipads with drones docked on each one. A grouping of antennas rose up at the rear of the roof. A Cummins turbocharged 600-horsepower engine that had been modified way beyond street-legal powered the vehicle.

The inside resembled a military command center, with a wall of monitors and a desk with multiple laptops. Bradford Travers, second in charge in Carmotte's organization, was in a leather seat toward the rear of the motor home. He was overseeing the contract and making sure everything went to plan.

Those duties included managing the assassins who signed on for the hit, as well as the scavies. He was also responsible for tracking Sei and updating the dossier. And lastly, he was responsible for making sure the reach of law enforcement didn't touch Carmotte. The responsibility was epic, and since his last few months' performances wasn't stellar, Travers was eager to please. He named his weapon on wheels Pegasus.

Also riding inside Pegasus with Travers were two skillful hackers: Duc Tran and Gil Rocha. Tran was a nineteen-year-old who had been recruited straight out of Vietnam. He'd been wreaking havoc on governments all over the world from his bedroom simply for fun. Carmotte had personally told Travers to hire the kid. Rocha was a Brazilian that Travers had worked with in the past. He trusted him, and plus, he needed someone more mature than the vaping Viet kid who liked to rap in his mother tongue.

Those two were there to monitor the chatter in the message boards and chat rooms in the dark web and on conventional social media platforms. If they needed, they could also hack into any public or private CCTV system. One of the large monitors featured a graphic of the United States with live weather and traffic updates. Travers could monitor all of the highways and roads as well as the railroads and bus lines. A flip of a switch, and he could see every plane in U.S. airspace.

Even though he hadn't received any confirmed sightings, he was sure Sei was still in the country. The previous night, she had left a mess at a gas station not far from Truckee, just west of the Nevada border. Travers assumed it was Sei because one of those individuals had registered. If he couldn't track Sei by sight, he'd follow her trail of bodies.

The one other person onboard Pegasus was the driver, who happened to also be Travers's personal driver. His name was Gary. You couldn't tell from his high school science teacher getup, but Gary was capable of anything from driving an M1 Abrams tank to drifting in a souped-up Nissan 350Z. Gary was the perfect getaway driver if they needed Pegasus to haul ass and get them out of a pickle.

"Gil, update the dossier," Travers said as he walked past,

heading to the front of the RV. "Sei's somewhere on Interstate 80. If she leaves another body, we'll know if she's heading East or West."

He settled in the passenger seat next to Gary. They were traveling east on Interstate 15, about an hour and a half outside of Las Vegas. "How long will it take for us to get to I-80?"

"I-15 intersects with I-80 in Salt Lake City. It'll take us about five hours if I drive the speed limit. I'll push it when I can, but there are too many speed traps along this route. I don't think you want to explain the getup we have in here to the Highway Patrol."

"Do what you can. Those bodies she left at the gas station happened sometime between nine and twelve last night. If Sei wasted no time and kept moving East, would she have already passed through Salt Lake City?"

"I'm guessing that distance from Truckee would take anywhere from seven to ten hours depending on what she's driving and traffic. Driving straight through, she'd be past Salt Lake City unless she stopped. But even she needs to sleep. If she was heading West, say to San Francisco, she'd be there by now. She really could be anywhere. She might have already anticipated being followed and got off I-80."

"Gary, you're not making me feel better."

"It's not my job to make you feel better. It's my job to drive."

"Well, try."

Travers studied the man who had been his personal driver for two decades. He was in his late fifties and always kept a neat and tidy buzz cut. He preferred sports coats and khaki pants instead of designer suits. Travers required everyone around him to dress professionally. The only exception he had ever made was for the two hackers. Gary's physical shape had softened in the last couple of years, but he was still the best driver Travers had ever come across, hands down. Lastly, Gary had a pretzel addiction. He always kept a bag nearby.

Gary cleared his throat. "I have a question. What happens if we end up finding her?"

"What do you mean?"

"I mean, what's the plan if we actually stumble across Sei? Forget about taking her down. Who in here is capable of taking her on? I'm talking about survival. I'm a driver. Those two guys back there are hackers. And I've known you for a long time. You're no Mike Tyson. I can't imagine Sei would happily join us for a bologna and cheese sandwich."

Travers leaned back in his chair and pondered what Gary had just said. The question he had brought up was something Travers had overlooked entirely. In his desperation to prove his worth to Carmotte by managing the contract, he never thought all of his chasings might land him the prize: Sei.

At five in the afternoon, the sun was nearing the horizon but the heat waves rising off the highway were still visible. Iron Wolf had combed I-80 all night and most of the following day. She assumed if Sei was on that highway, she would be somewhere between Truckee and Salt Lake City. That distance was 549 miles.

Word had spread quickly about her run-in with a couple of gang members near Truckee. Iron Wolf had ridden to the roadside gas station where it had gone down. Law enforcement was investigating the crime scene, so Iron Wolf kept her distance and observed. She figured Sei had stopped to gas up, which meant she intended to continue east. Iron Wolf got back on her bike and started looking for signs that Sei might have left on I-80.

Tracking someone was a slow and tedious process. Sei could have kept moving without slowing, or she could have made other stops along the highway. There was only one sure way to know: examine everything. That didn't mean Iron Wolf looked at everything. She had to put herself in Sei's shoes and sync to her state of mind.

Sei had just executed three people. Why would she stop?

could think of that would be roaming around the train tracks during the night were hobos.

Iron Wolf continued to examine the ground. No blood. No signs of a fight or a struggle. Iron Wolf knew this was Hobo Nation territory. *Do they not know about the contract?*

Further up ahead, she picked up multiple shoe prints, including Sei's, converging toward the tracks. *It looks like she went willingly with them. No way they captured her. She would have executed them all. What does she want with the hobos? Why are they playing along?*

The only explanation Iron Wolf could think of was that she needed their protection.

12

W hen I woke from my sleep, I found myself alone and
still on the sofa in Junks' dwelling. A bowl of hobo stew
was on a small table in front of me where I had left it. I glanced
at my watch, and to my surprise, discovered I had slept the
entire day. I reached around my back—I still had my handgun.
Just then, the door opened, and in walked Junks.

"You're up," he said.

"Why did you allow me to sleep all day?"

"You needed it."

"We wasted valuable time."

"I already told you, Sei, we travel at night. It's better for you.
As soon as the sun hides, we'll catch out."

"Will Cagey Mike be joining us?"

"He and a few trusted others."

"What business do you have in Britt, if you don't mind me
asking?"

"Hobo business. Talking about it will only bore you. I have
some last-minute dealings to take care of. We'll leave in exactly
one hour. I'll be back by then. There's a creek nearby. The
water's clean if you feel like splashing some on your face." Junks

picked up the flail he had shown me earlier. "Did you want to take this?"

"I'm fine with what I have."

He left carrying the flail.

After a few minutes of sitting by myself, I decided to take Junks' advice to freshen up. I exited the shack and squinted even though it was twilight. My eyes hadn't been exposed to the sun in almost twenty-four hours. There were more hobos in the jungle than I had remembered seeing when I arrived. No one bothered to look my way. I stopped a woman passing by.

"Excuse me," I said. "Which way is the creek?"

"It's over there," she pointed beyond two other shacks.

"Thank you."

I walked in that direction. A man yelling in the distance caught my attention. I looked back over my shoulder and saw a man on his knees. He had his hands steepled in front of him. Junks stood in front of the man, and the two of them were surrounded by other men. Junks swung the flail a second later, and the round sphere caved in the man's head. He slumped to the ground and remained motionless. I turned back and continued to the creek.

After a few minutes of walking, I heard the gurgling of water. A moment later, I came upon a crystal clear creek no more than fifteen feet across. I squatted near the edge and dipped a finger into the cold water. I slipped off my boots and hiked up my jeans to my calves before stepping in. The chilly water felt exhilarating and soothing, and the smooth pebbles making up the streambed felt nice against my feet. I wiggled my toes. They'd been cooped up in my overheated boots for a long time.

I stared at the mountains in the distance, wondering whether that was the source of the creek. I knelt down and scooped up a handful of water onto my face. I did that a few

times, enjoying the cool water as I felt my face tighten and reju-
venate on the spot.

I stood up and turned around to find Cagey Mike standing a
foot away from me. Instinctively my fist shot up, striking him in
his throat. Before he could gag, I'd swept him off his feet and
pounced on his chest. I twisted his mace out of his hand and
shoved the handle down against his throat.

"Sei!" a voice called out.

I looked up and saw Junks hurrying over to us.

"Let him go, Sei. I told Cagey Mike to come to get you."

I released the pressure from his throat and got up off of him.

"Crap, lady," he said, still choking for air. "What's your
problem?"

"Cagey Mike, it's my fault," Junks said. "I should have told
you not to approach Sei like that."

Junks reached down and helped the gasping man back up to
his feet.

"Shit, Junks. Next time fetch her yourself."

Junks gave Cagey Mike a comforting slap on the back. "I
will."

Junks watched Cagey Mike walk away. When he was far
enough away from us, Junks turned back to me. "I'm surprised
you didn't hear Cagey Mike coming up on you."

"Be thankful I didn't kill him."

"Are you feeling okay?"

"I'm fine. Did you need to inform me of something?"

"I wanted to talk to you alone before we were surrounded by
people. Remember when I mentioned the Indian reservations?"

I nodded.

"I thought they would remain neutral in this mess, but it
seems the bounty is too much to ignore. There's a good chance
we might be attacked during our journey."

"How do they know I'm here with you?"

"People talk, Sei. It can't be contained. We're leaving now. It's no longer safe to stay here. Also, I know I'm asking a lot, but could you tell Cagey Mike you're sorry? He's a good guy, and you'll want him watching your back."

Once back in the jungle, I sought Cagey Mike out. He flinched when I reached out to his neck.

"Are you okay?" I asked as I touched him gently.

This was the first time I was able to get a good look at the man. He had deep blue eyes that were constantly searching. The bruising on his neck wasn't that bad. He'd survive.

"Yeah, I'm fine."

I gave him a squeeze on his arm. That was the most he would get from me.

quickly becoming the only source of light. Sei wouldn't stay put for long. If she was in the camp, she was only waiting for nightfall to start traveling again.

Iron Wolf crouched and moved toward the next shack. She didn't hear anyone inside. She took a moment to study the camp from her new position when the crunch of footsteps suddenly caught her ear. A second later, a hobo rounded the corner of the shack.

Iron Wolf popped up from her squat and slammed her palm into the man's face, snapping his head back. He countered quickly with a hooking right and left, both catching air as Iron Wolf ducked twice. She kicked the man's feet out from under him, and he landed flat on his back, in pain. Iron Wolf pounced on top of his chest, slamming her hand down over his mouth to quiet him.

He bit down on one of her fingers. The leather riding gloves she wore softened the bite, but it still hurt like hell. Iron Wolf struck him repeatedly in the face with her other fist, and he let go. She raised her hand up high and, with all her might, slammed her fist into the man's throat. He gagged and choked. But Iron Wolf wasn't yet done.

Drawing her knife, she shoved it clear through his throat and severed his windpipe. A second later, she ripped his throat out. He was unable to breathe and unable to make any noise. Iron Wolf got up and stomped on him, knocking him unconscious.

Iron Wolf peeked around the shack in case her little rumble had drawn attention. It hadn't.

She slipped off the backpack she had been carrying and removed two Beretta M9A3s, excellent tactical handguns with double-stack magazines that took seventeen rounds. She screwed a silencer on each one.

From there, she studied the enclosed shacks. One of them

looked sturdier and a bit larger than the others. Was Sei staying in the nice one? Iron Wolf knew Junks was the leader of the Hobo Nation. It made sense that he'd have the best shack. Iron Wolf moved around the camp until she was crouched behind it. She placed her ear against the wood and heard soft music playing. She searched for any small crack or hole that would allow her to peek inside but didn't find one.

The sun had already dipped below the horizon, and night had settled in. Iron Wolf gripped the handles of the Berettas tighter. Now was the time to strike.

Iron Wolf emerged from the dark and into the camp. There were three hobos to the right sitting on buckets around a campfire. She fired, striking all three in the head. To the left, near the front of the target shack, stood another hobo guarding the entrance. He took a bullet to the forehead. Iron Wolf fired at other targets, dropping them to the ground as she quickly headed to the shack entrance.

The remaining hobos took up arms and attacked. One moved quickly toward Iron Wolf's flank with a raised spiked club. Iron Wolf fired twice into his chest before spinning around and narrowly avoiding a crushing blow from the club of another hobo. Iron Wolf countered with a snapping kick to the man's head, stunning him before firing multiple times at him.

Iron Wolf continued to make her way to the shack while fending off attacks. She kicked the door open and entered with both guns out in front. It was empty. Iron Wolf spun around and put down another hobo who came in after her.

Did I choose wrong?

Iron Wolf quickly exited the shack and ran to another. Inside she fired on four shadowed individuals. None were Sei.

She burst back out in the open and ducked below a swinging bat. Two shots to her attacker's gut and then one to the head before Iron Wolf moved toward the last shack. *Your time has come, Sei.*

Iron Wolf kicked through the flimsy door blind firing, but that shack was empty. Sei had already left the camp.

C agey Mike led the way to the small train depot. It was a fifteen-minute jog from the jungle. Junks, four of his inner circle, made up of three men and one woman, and I followed in single file until we reached the edge of the station.

We stopped near a chain-link fence that enclosed the train yard. There were no lampposts, so we were easily hidden. Up ahead, though, to the left side of the train station, lights attached to the small building lit up that section of the yard.

"Is that the train we're taking?" I asked as I pointed to ten boxcars on the track.

"No, the train we're taking is passing through the mainline," Junks answered. "We'll need to catch on the fly."

"There's a bull up there," Cagey Mike said.

"'Bull is railroad security," Junks whispered to me. "They're more of a bother than a threat."

"There's the train," Cagey Mike pointed.

Down the track, I could see the headlights, three in the shape of a triangle.

We slipped through a small hole in the chain-link fence and made our way toward the tracks.

"This train is loaded with open hopper cars. It's not ideal because we'll be sitting inside on top of whatever they're hauling. No cover."

"What's usually inside?" I asked.

"Rocks, coal, stuff like that, but I don't want to wait around for the next train. Hopper cars have a little porch in the front and back. That's where we'll climb onboard. From there, there's a ladder to climb inside the car. Got it?"

I nodded.

As the train neared, I could see the hopper cars that Junks had mentioned.

"This train is hauling a full load—twenty cars. We'll hop on the cars toward the rear."

We remained crouched in the shadows as the train slowly passed by. As the last of the cars approached, we made our move. Cagey Mike climbed up onto the porch first. He helped the other men up, and one by one, they climbed up a small ladder and into the hopper.

"You're next, Sei," Junks said.

I grabbed onto Cagey Mike's hand, and he pulled me up onto the porch. I climbed up the ladder and into the hopper full of sand. Junks was right behind me, followed by Cagey Mike.

"We got lucky," one of the hobos said. "This will make a comfortable ride." He was already burrowing himself into a small hole.

"Indeed," Junks said. "Settle in, Sei. We have a long ride ahead of us."

Junks and I moved to the front of the hopper, away from the others, so we could talk privately.

"How do you get updates while you're on the train?" I asked.

He produced a small mobile phone from his jacket. "I might be a hobo, but I got a phone." He smiled.

Junks switched the phone on. "I keep it off, so I don't drain the battery while we travel. Searching for signal sometimes drains the battery quick."

Once the phone had powered up, it chimed, and he checked the message. He quickly made a phone call.

"Doozer, it's Junks," he said as he covered his mouth over the phone. "What happened? Just now? How many? Get out of there." Junks disconnected the call. "A professional hit the jungle."

"Are you sure it wasn't a scavie?" I asked.

"Doozer was on his way back from the creek. He saw it all go down. One person—a woman. She wiped out everyone in the jungle. She was looking for you, Sei."

This was the second attempt I had by another assassin. They were the ones I had to be cautious with.

"Does he know who it was?" I asked.

"He said she looked Native American. Any ideas?"

"Just one: Iron Wolf."

"I haven't heard that name in years," Junks said. "This contract is bringing everyone back into the fold. I'll tell you right now, Sei, aside from my people, I can't guarantee anyone with Hobo Nation will be friendly with you, even if they know you're with me. After we part in Britt, you'll need to be extra careful. Sei...what's out east?"

"I have a friend who I believe can help me locate Ethan. If I can find him, I'll be able to end this."

"Good reason to go. I'll remind you again to stay away from the tracks east of the Mississippi River. The Wilds are a dangerous place. The hobos on those tracks will turn on their friends they've known for years. You don't need the added hardship."

"Besides I-80 in Indiana and the tracks, anything else I should be aware of?"

"Those are the only two problem spots I can think of. Sei, I don't understand why you don't just disappear for a year or two. Let this cool down. Everyone chasing you will get bored and move on. During that time, you can work on tracking down Ethan and strike when it's right."

Junks made a strong argument, but only because he was unaware of one thing: my daughter, Mui. As far as the world knew, my daughter was dead. She had a funeral and had been put to rest. I made sure everyone in my world knew that Ethan had been responsible for that. Not so that they would turn around and hate him, but because I needed everyone to believe she was dead.

Mui was staying with the only person I could trust to watch over her: the top FBI agent at the San Francisco headquarters, Abby Kane. Mui was living with Abby and her family. And while she was safe at the moment, I wasn't sure how long the ruse could be kept up. If word got out that she was alive, Ethan would put all his efforts into finding her. He wanted revenge and he wouldn't stop until he got it.

"I appreciate your thoughts on my situation," I said. "I did think to go underground, but the more I thought about it, the more I realized the contract would just pick up where it had left off as soon as I reared my head."

"You're probably right, Sei. There has never, ever been a contract with a payout this size attached to it. People will still be talking about this long after you and I are gone. A legend is being made. I hope you're the shining star, and Carmotte is the bitter loser."

"Thank you."

"I know you think Carmotte is the prize here—take him out, and the contract is void. I'm not saying that isn't true. It is, but if you want my advice, I think attacking the head of the snake right now will be very hard."

"What kind of advice is that to give? Ethan's death is the only death that really matters."

"I agree, but I think to do that, you need to weaken him first. Right now, loyal soldiers surround him. They're running interference while managing the day-to-day tasks. Carmotte is sitting comfortably from a safe place while he watches the show. The odds are, if I'm to be truthful here, you will meet your demise before he does."

"Are you making a suggestion or pointing out flaws?"

"You need to weaken him, Sei. Rather than putting all your energy and focus on finding a direct path to Carmotte, take out the people closest to him. I know you feel that time is not on your side, but this might be the better strategy going forward."

Junks had made a valid observation. In a hurry to eliminate the contract on my head by killing Ethan, I'd become too narrowly focused. I wasn't considering other strategies, like the one Junks had just pointed out. I'd developed tunnel vision. What Junks had proposed would take longer, but the upside was that Ethan's defenses would be weakened.

"I hadn't looked at it that way," I said. "It does make sense. His advantage is the wall he's built around himself. Rather than trying to scale it to get to him, you're suggesting I take out the doors that lead inside."

"That's right. Take out his lieutenants, and you'll have an easier chance of getting to him. Many people will come after you. It'll be impossible for you to fight them all off successfully, even someone with your talent. The odds will catch up with you. So the question now is, do you know any of his inner circle?"

"I believe I do. There were three men beside Ethan when I last encountered him. For them to be traveling directly with him could only suggest they are part of his inner circle. Very few people ever get that close. I only know the names of two, but I know what they all look like."

"Then you have a start. Take them out, and you'll have an easier time getting to Carmotte."

I thought more about Junks' proposal and tried to find holes or anything that would debunk that strategy, but it seemed sound. Ethan expected me to come directly for him. He wouldn't expect me to focus on his inner circle.

"How many reservations will we pass that worry you?" I asked, turning the conversation back to our current situation.

"There's a group of Native Americans that split off from the Ute Tribe. They spend most of their time around Cheyenne, Wyoming. They're a pack of misfits that are always looking for trouble. They travel on dirt bikes and love swinging those toma-hawk axes around. They used to be called Devil's Breath."

"What are they called now? Morning Breath?"

Junks smiled. "You can be funny when you want, Sei. Now they call themselves Aw, Fuck! They were terrorizing so many towns that people would say, 'Aw, fuck,' whenever they showed up. The name stuck. They're a nasty group. I don't think anyone would miss them if they were wiped clear off the face of this planet. We're out in the open," Junks motioned around us, "not much to separate us from them should they find us. Plus, the train is pulling a full load, so it won't be hard to keep up."

"But they would need to know we're on a train, and this one specifically. I imagine at any given moment there are dozens of trains on the tracks in this area."

"I think a lot of people are talking, and no one can be trusted. Everyone wants a piece of that bounty. We might have to defend this turf."

"How long before we reach Cheyenne?"

"Around noon tomorrow if the train continues without inter-ruption."

I wanted to ask Junks if he was tempted by the bounty but

I thought about calling my daughter, but I knew it was dangerous to do so. I missed her voice, and knowing our opportunities to talk would be sparse burned a hole in my heart.

You should know, this wasn't the first time I feared for my daughter's life more than I did mine. During her birth, I was led to believe she had died when in fact, she'd been kidnapped. I didn't discover the truth until two years later. It took me more than five years to find and rescue her.

Ethan was the second person to kidnap her. Rescuing her from him was the reason for my current situation. But understand, Mui isn't a defenseless teen girl. She was actually trained by another assassin, the man who first took her: The Black Wolf. He was a notorious assassin who wanted to groom my child into the ultimate weapon and have her be a part of his clan.

From age two to eight, Mui had been trained to be a lethal fighter. That training also went beyond weapons and hand-to-hand combat. She was taught how to track and infiltrate covertly as well as a slew of countermeasures. She was taught survival skills that could keep her alive in the mountains or the desert. She could hunt, trap, and build a shelter. I would say she was much better-rounded than I was. All she lacked was experience.

After rescuing her from the Black Wolf, I continued to train her for a bit longer, mainly to gauge her abilities. She knew enough to protect herself, so I stopped her training. I didn't want her to have my life: one of constantly looking over her shoulder. Even though I was no longer accepting contracts and had retired for all intents and purposes, one never really retires from this profession. I wanted Mui to have a normal life—a happy life without worry.

I had begun to wonder if that would ever be possible. Not because of her, but because of me. My past continued to attack the two of us. I couldn't delete it. It would always be there, waiting to strike and destroy whatever sense of normalcy we had managed to carve out for ourselves. Rather than wrestle endlessly with those thoughts, I accepted that I would simply have to tackle them as they came.

Junks woke as the sun had begun to rise and stretched his arms over his head.

"Did you sleep well?" I asked.

"Like a baby. Anything to report?"

"Nothing."

"I'll be back."

Junks crawled across the sand to his men and had a discussion with them. I wasn't bothered by the secrecy. I had my own concerns that took up plenty of bandwidth. Twenty minutes later, Junks crawled back over to me with a paper bag in his hand. He pulled out a bottle of water and handed it to me, along with an orange.

"Breakfast."

He had the same for himself. He also had two more oranges in the bag, a large bag of trail mix, a bag of beef jerky, a couple of energy bars, and extra bottles of water.

"This will have to hold us over until we get to Britt."

"Thank you. What about your men?"

"They have a stash as well."

Junks unscrewed his bottle of water and took a healthy swig before peeling his orange.

"You haven't asked, but I thought I'd bring it up," Junks said. "On the topic of the bathroom, normally we go off the side of a car or hold it. But we're in a sandbox here, so we would normally reserve the very middle as a toilet. I recommend you dig a hole in the corner over there when you need to go. I'll move away and give you some privacy." He pulled out a couple of small packets of tissue from the bag. "In case you need it."

Until Junks brought up the bathroom situation, I hadn't

given it any thought. I'd try my best to keep it to urination. The life of a hobo was interesting, to say the least.

We didn't talk much while we ate. Junks was content to fiddle with his flail, making sure it was in working order.

"What are the odds of interference in Cheyenne?" I asked.

"Fifty-fifty. Like you said earlier, there are a lot of trains, and we're zooming by. We might get lucky and have smooth riding all the way to Britt. You're ready to go if it turns out to be other-wise?" he asked as he glanced over at the handgun that I had sitting in my lap.

"I have twenty-four rounds plus the four throwing knives you gave me. It'll have to do until I can stock up."

"You making a run into Chicago?"

"There is someone I can reach out to in Nebraska, along the Missouri River. I want to see if I'm able to stock up there before deciding on Chicago."

Junks nodded. "You'll be able to get off the train in Omaha and follow the river."

Just then, Cagey Mike shouted, grabbing both our attention. He pointed off to the left side of the train.

"Aw, Fucks are coming."

About fifty yards away, I saw a pack of dirt bikes closing in. Each bike carried two men.

"Get ready, Sei," Junks said as he grabbed the handle of his flail. "They came with bigger numbers. They plan to board."

As the bikes neared our car, the details of the men were clearer. They were young, and the passengers on the bikes were waving tomahawks in the air. There were fifteen bikes, thirty men in total to deal with. There were only six of us.

The dirt bikes split. About half approached on the left while the rest came up on the right of our car.

"Hold the left!" Junks called out to his men. "We'll take the right!"

Junks and I made our way to the rear of the car. The Aw, Fucks didn't wait to board. A few drivers positioned their bikes near the car behind ours, and passengers climbed onto the train. A shot echoed.

Junks and I looked over our shoulders toward his men. One lay dead on the sand, his face destroyed by what I could only imagine had been a shotgun.

attack Junks and Cagey Mike. A screaming engine caught my attention, and I spun around in time to see a dirt bike from my side land on top of the car.

The men abandoned the bike and came straight at me, tomahawks raised above their heads. I fired, knocking both men down, and then focused on shooting the other two, but they were already engaged in battle with Junks and Cagey Mike.

I picked up a tomahawk and attacked the flank of the one nearest me. The blade of my tomahawk severed his right arm at the elbow. I then took his head clean off his shoulders. Junks and Cagey Mike demolished the other man.

I focused back on my side of the car. There were still three more bikes.

"How many on your side?" I called out to Junks.

"Four! They're backing off."

They'd lost half of their crew. And it was just Junks, Cagey Mike, and me left. Junks had lost three of his trusted men and launched himself into an angry tirade, tossing the dead members of the Aw, Fucks right off the car, along with their dirt bikes. He then pounded his fists again and again into the sand.

"Let him go," Cagey Mike said. "He needs to release his frustration. Go grab your gear. We're moving to the last car. The Aw, Fucks might regroup and come back."

I retrieved my backpack, as well as Junks' belongings. Cagey Mike and I hopped over to the next car and continued until we reached the last one. We dug ourselves into the sand near the rear.

"Is he always like that?" I asked.

Cagey Mike nodded. "He takes it personally like he failed them, especially Wella. He's known her for a long time. He'll be all right. He just needs time alone."

I noticed Cagey Mike's hands were shaking.

"Are you okay?"

He glanced at his hands. "I've gotten into my fair share of fights over time, but they were just fights. No one died."

"Is this your first time?" I asked.

"Second."

"It's understandable."

"Was it hard for you? I mean when you first killed some-one?" he asked.

"Talking about it will make it harder."

He nodded and stopped his questioning.

17

Travers had gotten word about the attack at the hobo camp in Nevada and ordered Gary to get them there as quickly as possible. He wanted a firsthand look at what had happened and to see if there was anything he could learn about Sei's travel plans. The more he could share with his legions of hired guns, the better the chances of someone putting her to rest. As far as they knew, law enforcement wasn't even aware of the situation at the hobo camp.

"We're entering the town of Carlin," Gary said, "The location of the camp isn't accessible by vehicle. From the train station, it's about a twenty-minute walk into the brush before you reach it."

"That's fine," Travers said. He looked over at Tran. He had his eyes closed and was rapping to himself. "I'll take Gil with me. Just let me know if the police start to swarm."

It was hot out, so Travers changed out of his suit and into jeans and a polo shirt before they exited the motor home.

"What are we looking for?" Rocha asked as they marched into the brush.

"I want to see if what happened here is true. Secondly, we're looking for anything that might give us a clue to where Sei is heading."

The sun beamed directly down on the two men. Their shirts quickly developed wet spots as sweat bubbled across their arms and faces. They knew they were on the right track when the smell of rotting flesh filled the air.

They slowed their pace as they came upon the camp; both already had handguns drawn. The buzz of flies grew louder with every step. Travers led the way between two shacks and stopped. Laid out before them were at least a dozen bloated bodies frozen into unnatural shapes with the onset of rigor mortis.

"Holy shit. They look like discarded mannequins," Rocha said quietly as he pulled the front of his shirt over his nose. "And it fricking reeks."

"Search those shacks over there," Travers said. "I'll search the ones over here."

The bodies in the shacks were just as smelly and stiff. Travers looked over everything in each shack, including the bodies. So far, nothing jumped out at him. When he met up with Rocha on the other side of the camp, neither reported anything.

"You really think she did all this?" Rocha asked. "I mean, how can one person kill so many people? And it's not like they weren't armed. Clearly, they were."

"They had clubs. She had a gun. Almost every dead guy I looked at had a gunshot wound to his head. But to go one step further, she is dangerous. It took me a while to realize this. Don't ever underestimate her or any of the psychos chasing her. Some of them are just as deadly."

"Well, assuming she was here, the question is why did she attack the hobo camp?" Rocha asked. "It's not like she stumbled across it. She either came here purposely or was brought here by someone, right? I mean, that makes the most sense to me."

"Yeah, something isn't adding up here," Travers said. "It makes no sense to come here and wipe out an entire camp of hobos. What does she get out of it? It's to her advantage to stay under the radar. This is the complete opposite."

"Could another assassin have caught up with her? It's not like they would report it to us. It takes away their advantage, right?"

"You're right. It does. They're not required to do anything anyway. The hobos were friendly, and one of our registered contestants playing along caught up with her."

"She got away, then."

"She did, but she's with hobos, and what is it that hobos do?"

"They ride trains."

The two men hurried back to the motor home parked near the train station. Travers took a quick look around the building and spied security cameras.

"We need to hack into their system," he said.

"No problem," Rocha said. "We should be able to do that easily."

Back inside the motor home, Rocha and Tran quickly hacked into the security system, giving them access to the stored footage. Travers and Gary stood hovering over their backs. Two camera angles were pointing in opposite directions on the tracks. Tran took the east-facing camera, Gil started on the west-facing camera.

After the first hour of combing the footage, they'd only gone back in time to nine in the morning.

"How far back do you think we need to look?" Gary asked.

"At least until sunset the previous day."

"That'll take a while," Rocha said.

"Do we want to sit here or keep moving?" Gary asked. "Maybe at least head back to Salt Lake City."

"Yeah, let's do that. No need to stick around this town any longer. It's clear she's moving east."

Gary fired up the motor home and got back on Interstate 80, driving east toward Salt Lake City. So far, neither Rocha nor Tran had found anything in the footage. When they reached Salt Lake, Travers and Gary left the motor home to pick up food and supplies while Rocha and Tran searched through the footage.

"Anything?" Travers asked when he and Gary returned.

Both men shook their heads. They had now searched back to around eleven o'clock the night before.

"At the rate they're moving, it'll take about another three hours or so before they get to footage of the previous sunset," Gary said. "Maybe we keep heading east, but at a slower pace."

"Yeah, let's do that," Travers answered.

About an hour and a half later, Rocha shouted, "I got something. Look, here." Rocha pointed at his screen. Travers came up behind him and looked over his seat. "You can barely make it out, but it looks like a group of people running to this train."

"Can you take that section and brighten it somehow?" Travers asked.

"Yeah, hold on."

Rocha copied that part of the footage and transferred it into another app on his laptop. He adjusted the colors, and the blobs became more human-like.

"Those are definitely people," Travers said, "and it looks like they're hopping on that train. There's got to be identification markers on those cars. Find them."

"Here it is." Rocha wrote the numbers down. "We have a timestamp for when this train passed through the station. We should be able to locate the route."

"You need to hack into Union Pacific?" Travers asked.

"Maybe not. The schedule might already be published."

Rocha did a quick search for public information on train schedules for Union Pacific. There were several system maps listed for the public. Still, none of them provided the information they would need to track this particular train.

"We'll have to hack in," Rocha said.

Between Rocha and Tran, they were able to gain access to Union Pacific in thirty minutes.

"The train is heading east along the I-80 corridor," Rocha said. "It's scheduled to stop in Des Moines, Iowa...switching cars. It doesn't say where it's heading after that."

"Where is it now?" Travers asked.

"I'm sure there's a way UP is tracking their trains via GPS, but we don't seem to have access to it right now. We'll need time to find a way."

"What cities will the train be passing through? There must be a way to deduce where it is."

"Hold on," Rocha said. "Now, mind you, this is all a guesstimate, but if my math and timing are right, the train just passed through the rail yard in North Platte, Nebraska. The next major rail yard is in Omaha, Nebraska."

"So between North Platte and Omaha." Travers clapped his hands. "Great. Update the dossier. Tell everyone what train Sei is on, where it's heading, and what town it'll pass through next. Gary, get us to Omaha ASAP."

18

Junks remained alone for almost an entire hour before joining us in the last car. Neither Cagey Mike nor I broached the subject of our fallen friends.

"How much ammo do you have left?" Junks asked me.

"Three rounds."

He placed a tomahawk next to me. "You should take this. It might come in handy until you're able to resupply. I hope your contact in Omaha works out for you."

"So do I. If it doesn't, I'll keep on moving."

"I know earlier I said I didn't want to know where you were heading, but I'm curious. You're risking a lot to get there."

"I'm heading to New York."

"That's a dangerous place to go."

"Willie's there."

Junks' eyes popped open. "Willie? Now that's a name I haven't heard in years. How is he doing?"

"He's a little older but fine."

"I can see why you're heading there. He probably is your best bet at tracking down Carmotte."

"And I can trust him."

"That you can. It's been a long time since he and I have spoken. Tell Willie I said hello and that I wish him good health."

"I'll do that. I want you to know that I'm grateful for everything you've done for me. I'm sorry about the others."

"This is the life we live, Sei."

"I know, but I still want to say thank you. If you ever need my help, I'm here."

Junks chuckled. "Survive this contract, and then we can talk about payback."

WE ARRIVED in Omaha in the early evening without any further incidents, which pleased us all. The train was directed off the main tracks into the yard.

"It looks like they're switching cars," Junks said. "We'll all need to get off."

"What will you do?" I asked.

"It's no bother. We'll catch out on the next train, or if this one is ready before that, we'll hop back on. And you?"

"I need transport."

"You shouldn't have a problem finding something. It's still early in the night."

Once the train came to a complete stop, we climbed off. Junks escorted me safely out of the yard while Cagey Mike stayed behind.

"Are you familiar with Omaha?" Junks asked.

"Not really."

"There are taxis outside of the train station, if that makes it easier for you. I recommend you take one. The road outside will take you straight into town. There are a ton of used car lots along the way."

"Thank you."

Junks gave me a hug with a pat on the back and left quickly. I made my way to the front of the train station and climbed into a taxi.

On the way into town, I kept watching for the car lots. Junks had mentioned many big ones selling new and used cars. I wanted a small independent dealer that wouldn't draw attention and, more importantly, that would accommodate my demands.

"Stop here, please," I said.

I paid the taxi driver and exited, then walked a few yards back to the driveway with a sign above it that read: #1 Car Stop. It definitely had that independent dealership look: cars lined up and facing the road, older compact models. But what caught my eye was parked further back near a mobile office trailer: a black Kawasaki sport bike. Hanging off the handlebar was a yellow sign with black numbers: $1,999.

I didn't see a salesperson, so I knocked on the door to the trailer. I heard footsteps before the door swung inwards, revealing a man wearing jeans, a checkered shirt, and a beige cowboy hat. He looked to be in his mid-fifties and had a potbelly.

"Can I help you?"

"I'm interested in this bike."

The man looked me up and down and then at the bike. "It's a little too much bike for a woman your size. How about that Volkswagen Beetle?"

"I want the bike. Does it run well?"

"Yeah, it runs fine."

"That price is fine with me," I said.

"All right, come inside. I'll get you set up."

The inside of the trailer looked exactly how I had imagined it would: wood paneling, linoleum floors, a metal desk covered with stacks of paperwork. Four metal filing cabinets ran along one wall. A painting of buffalo on the open range hung behind the desk. The man sat behind the desk, and I took a seat in one of the metal folding chairs in front.

"Just need to fill out paperwork, and we'll have you on your way. Are you from Omaha?"

"I'm not. And I'm also not interested in paperwork. I'll pay double if you hand over the keys right now."

He looked up with a crinkled brow. "What's that?"

"I said I'll triple the asking price if you hand over the keys right now."

He eyed me for a few moments. "Are you in trouble?"

"No. I'm in a hurry." I slipped off my backpack, removed six thousand dollars from inside, and placed it on the desk. "Do we have a deal?"

"The dealer plates are only good for thirty days. After that, if you get pulled over by the police, they'll impound the bike for no registration or proof of insurance."

I said nothing.

"Okay, suit yourself." He stood and opened a metal chest that sat on one of the filing cabinets. He handed me the keys to the bike.

"Give me a minute, and I'll fetch a gas container and top off your fuel tank for you."

"I appreciate that. Do you have a helmet to spare?"

"I'll see what I can come up with."

About twenty minutes later, I had a bike with a full tank of gas and a helmet on my head. I fired up the bike, gave the engine a few revs. Everything seemed to be in working order. I switched on the headlight and took off.

19

I rode north on Highway 74 toward the village of Decatur. I estimated it would take an hour and a half and put me there around ten at night. That didn't bother me, because my destination was the Black Crow Casino. One might question my reasoning for visiting a casino owned by Native Americans after being attacked by a gang of them, but the Omaha tribe that operated this casino was not associated with the Aw, Fucks.

The casino was located just outside of Decatur on a white riverboat that had three decks and a large paddle wheel in the rear. I pulled into a half-empty parking lot; it was a Wednesday night, so I expected the crowds to be minimal. I parked my bike away from the entrance, exchanged my helmet for a ball cap and headed inside.

At the entrance was a map of the boat. The first floor was reserved for gaming. There was a restaurant and more gaming on the second floor. A bar and a lounge area occupied the top deck. Once inside, I made my way to the cashier's cage and exchanged three hundred dollars for chips. I asked for two black chips, a hundred dollars each, one five-dollar chip, which was red, and the remaining money in silver dollars.

With my white bucket filled with coins, I walked over to the craps table, where I spotted the pit boss talking to a dealer. I took the two black chips out of my bucket and sandwiched a red chip between them, and when he broke away from his conversation with the dealer, I approached him.

"I have a special hand I'd like to play." I handed him the chips.

He looked me up and down before taking the chips from me and walking away. The chip sandwich I gave him would buy me access to my supplier, a Swedish man named Ivan. The tribe allowed him to conduct business there for a cut of his dealings.

I sat at an empty bank of slot machines that faced a wall, away from the main floor. These were dollar video poker machines, and the locals were busy pumping money into the rows of nickel slots. The casino wasn't that big, so the rows of video poker and slots were packed in tightly. The open area was a mix of blackjack, craps, baccarat, and roulette tables. The lounge next to the bar doubled as a sportsbook.

While I waited, I tried my luck with video poker while checking my watch every now and then.

Ten minutes.

Fifteen minutes.

At the thirty-minute mark, a cocktail waitress had stopped by and told me Ivan knew I was waiting and it wouldn't be much longer. The same cocktail server stopped by at the hour mark and apologized but repeated the same message.

It wasn't uncommon to wait; Ivan could be busy with another customer who may not know what he wants or be demanding to please. But that night I was on the clock. The longer I remained in that casino, the longer it would take to reach New York. Staying idle also increased the odds of me being attacked.

The bells and chimes of the machines continued to ring out,

but there was something strange about it. I glanced over my shoulder and realized most of the patrons had cleared out. It wasn't that late, eleven-thirty, but primarily locals visited this place, so maybe it wasn't entirely out of the ordinary. Still, I was on alert.

Dealers were shutting down their empty tables, and the cocktail servers had disappeared. The casino was open twenty-four hours, so it wasn't closing. I slipped off my stool and walked over to the craps tables. The croupiers were clear of customers and shutting down.

"Excuse me, where's the pit boss?"

"He'll be back shortly," one of them, a woman, answered.

"Does it always empty out around this time?"

"Depends. Tomorrow's a workday. We'll get busy around three or four in the morning as the early birds fly in."

I watched both of the croupiers walk towards a closed door manned by a guard with shifty eyes. I reached under my jacket, drew my handgun, and located a security camera to wave it at. I knew I was being watched. I walked around the casino floor and found it void of any customers and employees. I walked over to the entrance and discovered the doors had been chained shut. Either Ivan was taking a crack at the contract, or he sold me out.

"Sei!" A woman's voice called out.

I quickly moved away from the doors and into a row of video poker machines.

"Where are you?" the same voice called out. It was coming from the direction of the gaming tables.

I crouched as I moved down the aisle. I heard the roulette table spin. When I reached the end of the aisle, I stuck my head out. Standing next to a roulette table was Iron Wolf.

20

Travers was sitting up front with Gary when the motor home crossed the city limits into Omaha.

"What now, boss?" Gary asked.

"I'm not sure. Maybe we—"

"No way!" Tran shouted with a Vietnamese accent. "Come look. This her?" he asked in broken English.

Travers hopped out of his seat and ran back to where the two hackers were sitting. Up on Tran's screen was video footage of the inside of a casino. Crouched between video poker machines was a woman with black hair.

"Physically, it looks like her, but I need a good look at her face. Who uploaded this video?" Travers asked.

"This a live stream," Tran said.

"What? This is happening right now? Find that damn casino!"

Both hackers went to work while Travers watched the video.

"Come on, Sei. Look up. Let me see your face."

The woman glanced up at the camera a moment later, and a smile grew on Travers's face.

IRON WOLF WAS LOOKING in another direction. I raised my handgun and took aim. Just as I pulled the trigger, she dropped down.

"Sei, do you think it'll be that easy?" Iron Wolf said. "It's just you and me here. It's an even playing field."

"The cameras are watching me and providing you with intel," I said. "How else would you have known to duck?"

Iron Wolf laughed. "You're right. But I do want to be fair. I want to see what you're made of. I'll take my earpiece out."

A few seconds later, I saw a small object bounce off the top of a roulette table.

"How do I know you don't have one in each ear?"

"You'll have to trust me."

I had two rounds left. I knew I could hit Iron Wolf if given a chance. I moved toward the other end of the aisle and peeked around the corner. Iron Wolf fired, and I pulled back just in time to avoid a blast from a sawed-off shotgun.

I ran back toward the other end to flank her and caught the tail end of her ducking behind the other end of the video poker machines. I dove under a nearby craps table as another shotgun blast hit the top of the table.

I popped up on the other side. Iron Wolf was out in the open, walking toward me. I fired just as she dived down next to a blackjack table. I dropped down flat to the floor, looking for her legs, but the blackjack table had a solid base.

Where did she go?

A second later, a shadow passed across my face. Iron Wolf stood above me. A second later, she kicked my handgun out of my hand. I spun around, kicking her feet out from under her just as she fired her shotgun. The blast shattered the lights above, and glass rained down on us.

I swung my boot around toward her head, but she deflected it with her shotgun. In seconds we were both on our feet. Iron Wolf shot forward with a combination of fist strikes. My forearms took the brunt of the impacts, but one of her fists slipped through and landed clean on my nose. I felt the warm blood dribble out.

"She bleeds," Iron Wolf said.

I delivered a snapping kick to her outer thigh before unleashing my own combination of punches and kicks. Iron Wolf was adept at hand-to-hand combat. She deflected most of my attacks, but my kicks were wearing her down. I alternated between her thighs and the sides of her torso.

Iron Wolf countered by trying to snatch my throat. I caught her by the wrist and twisted, hoping to dislocate her elbow, but she jumped and twirled in the same direction, breaking free.

I moved in with a knee strike to her face, followed by an elbow to the back of her head, and she fell down to the floor. I raised a leg to stomp the back of her head, but she was quicker, snatching a piece of broken glass and puncturing my outer thigh. It didn't go in very deep, but it hurt like hell.

My leg buckled, and Iron Wolf popped back to her feet, her face bloodied from my knee strike.

"I will rip your throat out," she growled before attacking me.

We traded punches and kicks, both connecting with each other. Iron Wolf was able to counter more of my strikes than I had anticipated. It took everything I had to deflect most of her strikes, but she was still breaking through my defenses. I reached for the tomahawk I had tucked into my belt under my jacket.

Iron Wolf saw my move and kicked my hand away. I reached again, and she kicked it away again. Twice more, I tried, and both times her heavy boot slammed into my hand. A sharp pain rocketed up my arm from her last kick.

I ducked, avoiding her right hook, and retaliated with a straight punch to her chest, backing her up and causing her to choke on her breath. Her eyes darted to the shotgun on the floor, and she dived toward it. So did I.

Our bodies crashed into each other as we fought to lay hands on the weapon first. I grabbed Iron Wolf by the back of her head and slammed her face down onto the floor, but she connected with a sharp elbow to my head, stunning me. By the time I refocused, Iron Wolf had disappeared, and so had the shotgun.

I looked around for my handgun but didn't see it anywhere. I removed the tomahawk from my belt. I'd have to make the best of it.

"Sei," Iron Wolf called out playfully. "Miss me?"

I stood up and looked over to where I'd heard her voice: blackjack tables near a row of video poker machines. I spotted the top of her head barely poking above one of the tables.

I ran toward her and leaped upon the table, wanting to crack her head open with my tomahawk. But she'd already left the spot.

I leaped up onto the top of the row of video poker machines and spotted her running down the next aisle over. I jumped to the top of the next row, but she had already moved out of the aisle. I jumped down, figuring she had already reloaded her shotgun. I could either go right or left. I heard the soft pitter-patter of steps, and it sounded like they were heading left. I ran in that direction and raised my tomahawk, looking to connect with Iron Wolf at the end of the aisle. But when I rounded the corner, she wasn't there.

I looked down the next aisle over, and it was empty. I looked down the aisle I had just come from, and Iron Wolf fired her shotgun at me.

The liquor bottles on the shelf above the bar exploded. I

dropped to my butt with my back up against the row of video poker machines. I peeked back around the corner, and she'd disappeared again. Iron Wolf could flank me from either direction.

"What happened to your gun, Sei?" Iron Wolf called out. "Did you lose it already?"

She was to the rear of me, probably using the other side of the row as cover. I was too low to the floor to look over the top of the bar and use what was left of the mirrored shelving to see into the aisles. I slowed my breathing and listened carefully, hoping to pick up any sort of movement. I ran the layout of the casino through my head, looking for possible approaches to my position. How would Iron Wolf try to finish the job?

Left aisle?

Right aisle?

She knew where I was, but even she could only move down one aisle at a time, unless... *She's not on the floor!*

I shot up to my feet, spun around, and chucked the tomahawk as hard as I could. Walking along the top of the video poker machines was Iron Wolf.

Thunk!

The tomahawk struck her square in her face. She wobbled for a second before toppling off the top of the machines and landing on the floor. A leg stiffened before relaxing and falling to the floor. I snatched the shotgun from her and searched her body for any remaining shells.

I yanked the tomahawk out of Iron Wolf's face and made my way over to the door I had seen the employees walk through earlier.

"Ivan!" I shouted as my eyes settled on one of the security cameras above me.

I hacked at the doorknob until I broke it off. I headed to a Tintersection ahead and turned left. At the end of that hall was Ivan's office.

"Open up, Ivan!" I called out when I had reached it.

"It wasn't me, Sei! I was ordered. You got to believe me," he cried out from the other side.

The door was reinforced, and I couldn't breach it with the weapons I had.

"Supply me, and we'll call it even. Refuse, and I'll come back. You know I will."

A few moments passed before the door unlocked and swung inward. Peeking out from behind it was Ivan.

"I swear, Sei. Why would I screw with you?"

I pushed my way in. "I need weapons. Now!"

21

T he dark web exploded with activity over the livestreaming of Sei and Iron Wolf battling. Travers couldn't believe he had front row seats to a death battle.

"You're recording this, right? Right?" he asked.

Rocha nodded. "We're getting it all."

Travers was obviously Team Iron Wolf. If the assassin could put Sei down, and in front of everyone who mattered during a livestream, what a prize he could bring to his boss, Carmotte.

"This is like the UFC but with weapons," Rocha said. "Can you imagine how much money this fight would make if it was a pay-per-view event? Gazillions!"

"I like Sei. She hot," Tran said.

"Be careful where you say that, because the man who pays your salary wants her dead," Travers said.

The battle drew more viewers by the second. Odds were quickly established, and wagers were placed on the outcome. Individuals could not only bet on who would win, but how the kill would actually happen. Would it be fast and direct, or slow and painful? Bets could even be made on whether Sei would lose a limb from a shotgun blast. Most bets placed on Sei wagered Iron Wolf would take a tomahawk to the chest.

"I find it," Tran said. "She in this town." Tran zoomed in on an area north of Decatur, Nebraska. "This a casino."

"Gary, get us to the Black Crow Casino, north of Decatur. It's off Highway 75 along the Missouri River."

BECAUSE OF THE LIVESTREAM, Travers already knew Iron Wolf was dead, and Sei had fled the premises. Two individuals had won a big jackpot by taking the worst odds of them all: Iron Wolf would take a hatchet to the face. By the time the motorhome reached the casino, Travers had already updated the dossier with the latest information. Still, it wasn't like the people chasing the contract didn't see the live stream.

Gary stopped the motor home a few yards from the entrance of the casino. The parking lot was empty, save for a few vehicles. Law enforcement wasn't clued in just yet. Travers had done the research and knew the Omaha Tribe owned the casino. He also learned who the tall white guy with the weapons cache was: Ivan Ulfsson.

"You think the tribe officials are already in there trying to figure out how fucked they are?" Gary said. "I'm pretty sure Ivan was behind the livestream and not them. Livestreaming a death match can't end well for them. They'll need to pay a lot of officials off to make that go away."

"I don't know, and I don't care."

Travers tucked a handgun into the waistband of his pants before slipping on his suit jacket. "I'll be back."

"You sure you want to go in there? That livestream can flip on at any time."

"I want to talk to Ivan. I want to know what was said between them."

Gary lowered his voice. "Send the young one in to get Ivan. It's better."

"Duc! Up front and center now," Travers called. "Come on, chop, chop."

Tran made his way to the front of the motor home.

"Take this," Travers handed him the gun. "Go in there, find Ivan, bring him to me. Think you can handle that?"

"No problem. What if he don't come. I cap him?"

"No, I need him alive."

"I shoot his arm."

"Fine, just don't kill him. Understood?"

Travers and Gary watched Tran walk into the casino. Twenty minutes later, Tran appeared with Ivan right behind him.

"Is Ivan bleeding?" Gary said as he squinted. "Look at his arm."

A few seconds later, the door to the motor home opened. "Go!" Tran shouted.

A second later, Ivan stepped inside—he had been shot in the arm.

"Ivan, welcome. My name is Bradford Travers. I'm the shepherd of the contract on Sei's head. I trust you heard of it and the person who ordered the hit?"

Ivan was shaking uncontrollably. "Yes."

"Good. Don't worry, this won't take long, you'll be free to take care of your arm shortly. I want to know what you and Sei discussed."

"What do you mean?"

"There were words exchanged between you two. I want to know what was discussed verbatim."

"She needed weapons."

"Yes, I gathered that, but there seemed to be a little more discussion than 'I need weapons.' Did she say where she was going or what she was doing next?"

"She said she would kill me if I didn't cooperate."

"Why is this conversation feeling like I have to extract this information out of you? Just tell me, or else I will kill you."

"Weapons. That's what she wanted from me. If I didn't let her take what she wanted, she said she would kill me."

Travers tilted his head to the side as he pondered what Ivan had just said. "You know, I find it hard to believe that she said that. She doesn't really need to threaten you to get what she wants. She can just take it. You, I, we all saw what she is capable of. So one more time, what did she really say?"

"I asked her about her usage. Did she envision herself in close-quarters combat, or would she be out in the open and need a sniper rifle or explosives."

"Now see, that wasn't so hard, was it? Continue."

"She chose weapons that were covert and suited for close-quarters combat. Handguns with suppressors, titanium throwing knives, a garrote...the usual assassin load."

"And?"

"And I asked if she envisions herself in an urban setting or outdoors like a dense, wooded area."

"And?"

"She said urban. That's it. I swear."

"I believe you, that would be stupid of her to mention that, but there must be something else. Think, Ivan, your life is depending on it."

"Those were all the weapons she took and...."

"And what?"

"I had a bag of firecrackers. She wanted them."

"Firecrackers? Why did she want them?"

"I don't know."

"Were they aerials?"

"No, they were just those red firecrackers that explode on the ground and make a lot of noise. I told her they were old. She said she didn't care. He would appreciate them."

"He? Who is he?"

"She didn't say. I'm not sure if she even said that. Everything happened fast. I just agreed, so she would leave."

"Did Sei realize her fight with Iron Wolf was livestreamed?"

Ivan nodded.

"Why did you decide to livestream the fight?"

"She wanted me to... Iron Wolf told me to do it. She was positive she would win, and she said not to worry about the Omaha Tribe and that she would deal with them. She was going to cut me in on the bounty. It was too much money to turn down." Ivan took a moment to look at all the monitors. "Um, you said you were the shepherd of the contract, right? Shouldn't I at least be privy to a finder's fee? I livestreamed Sei. I think that's the first confirmed sighting of her."

Travers turned to Gary. "Can you believe this? He wants a finder's fee. Okay, Ivan. Since you did, in fact, put Sei at a location, you do deserve something for your efforts. Would you mind stepping outside for a moment? Duc, please escort Ivan out. You know what to do."

A few seconds later, there was a gunshot, and Tran stepped back into the motor home, alone.

"You think that was a smart thing to do?" Gary asked as he started the engine. "Maybe he still had information he was holding back on."

"Ivan gave me all the information I needed to figure out where Sei is heading."

"Yeah? And where's that?"

"New York City. That's where she was last time."

"What do firecrackers have to do with New York?" Gary asked.

"Chinatown."

22

I heeded Junks' advice and avoided all of Interstate 80 that cuts through Illinois and Indiana. I decided to take Interstate 64 across the rest of the country to Richmond, Virginia. I would lose time heading north to New York from Richmond. That would add an extra five hours of travel time. Not ideal.

It was also impossible for me to drive to Richmond nonstop. I would need to rest in a motel along the way, during daylight. I powered ahead through the night, doing my best to put as much distance between the casino and myself. I had left Ivan alive. I questioned whether that was smart or not. The old Sei would have dispatched him. He had admitted to me that he had contacted Iron Wolf but was only directed to do so by members of the Omaha Tribe.

Ivan was required to receive approval from the tribal council on every sale he made. So when they discovered I was on the property, they decided to capitalize on it. I wasn't sure who Ivan was more afraid of: the tribe or me. They must have had their hooks deep into him. But seeing that I let him go, he had made the right decision at the time.

I got as far as Louisville, Kentucky, when fatigue set in. It was ten in the morning, and I pulled into the first roadside motel I found and checked into a room. Before lying down, I quickly stitched up the wound Iron Wolf had given me using a suture kit I kept on me. After, I sent Willie a message in the chat room he'd set up to let him know my status. It was against the rules, but I felt like I needed to send word to him.

Willie had always been a stickler about communication. He understood that no matter how hard a person tried, they always left breadcrumbs. And that included him. But because of my particular situation, he had created a chat room in the dark web that only he and I had access to.

I hadn't communicated with him since leaving San Francisco, and I also hadn't received an update regarding his search efforts for Carmotte. I was curious, to say the least. But part of my reason for reaching out was to let him know I was still alive and on my way to him. I didn't mention my location in case the chat room was hacked. It was understood that all communication between us would remain generic and nebulous. Only he and I would ever know what we were talking about.

I waited a bit, but there was no answer. I stuck the back of the chair up against the doorknob, shut the drapes, and lay down on the bed. I woke later in the day feeling much better. I freshened up in the bathroom and then ate a tuna fish sandwich from the convenience store across the street before getting back on the highway.

Richmond was my next stopping point, eight hours away. I could rest there before making the final five-hour drive to New York during the night. If not, I'd have to stay the following day and try the next night. Or risk traveling by day.

All I wanted to do was get to New York so Willie and I could locate Ethan. The sooner I could make that happen, the sooner I could put this contract behind me. However, there was one catch working with Willie. He was putting his life in danger.

By poking around the web, Willie would, unfortunately, leave crumbs. He was good at hiding, but there's always a footprint left. If someone found out Willie was looking for Ethan, they could very easily connect the two of us. Willie wasn't an assassin; he was an information guru. It was in my best interest, for myself and as a friend, to ensure his safety. He was literally risking his life. I had made a promise to Willie that no harm would come to him. And that was a promise I intended to keep.

23

Undisclosed Location

Ethan Carmotte sat quietly in the leather chair behind a large wooden desk. He was dressed in an untucked white dress shirt and khakis. He had combed his silver hair back with his hands. He stared at a flat-screen that hung on the wall. Playing out before him was a replay of the fight between Sei and Iron Wolf. He had a smile stretched across his face and a twinkle in his blue eyes. He hadn't said a single word since he'd begun watching the video. His demeanor conveyed his thoughts: unabated joy.

"Wonderful. Absolutely wonderful," he said. "Let's watch it again. I want to soak in the details."

And that was precisely what happened.

Carmotte watched the video repeatedly, often pausing to replay certain scenes, especially the one where Iron Wolf took a hatchet to her face.

"Look at that. The way Iron Wolf moves across the top of the video machines. You can see the smugness dripping from her face. She really thought she had Sei, and then bam! Her face splits open. Marvelous. I do love that about Sei, her ability to counter when it's least expected. You have to appreciate that. Am I right?"

Sitting next to Carmotte was a bald man with a noticeable scar running across his chin. His name was Kazmer. He'd first come to work for Carmotte a few years ago. He was tasked with overseeing a job in Slovakia. By all accounts, it was meant to be a one-time thing. At the time, Carmotte wasn't even aware that Kazmer was working for him. He didn't waste time involving himself with those details, trusting his second in command, Bradford Travers, to handle those matters.

Travers oversaw all hiring and managed anyone who worked for Carmotte's organization. Kazmer had impressed Travers by proving himself adept at not only doing what Carmotte had asked but also taking it one step further and over delivering. It prompted Travers to introduce the Hungarian assassin to Carmotte.

From that point forward, with every job, Kazmer continued to gain Carmotte's trust and a place within his inner circle.

"She has a very unique way of handling situations," Kazmer said with an Eastern European accent.

"That she does. I never tire of watching her in action. Sadly, that doesn't forgive the hatred I have for that woman. Such a waste of talent."

Kazmer never asked any personal questions, settling on whatever Carmotte gave up during his countless ramblings. But over time, he'd learned enough about Carmotte's past with Sei. He'd been in love with the woman, probably the only time in his life. When she left him and disappeared, he could take it no other way but as an act of betrayal. Over time, Kazmer figured his boss's frail ego had become bitter, turning his sadness into anger, which only one thing would ever quell: vengeance. Only Sei's death would ever heal the wounded man.

"I wish I had watched it live." Carmotte snapped his fingers. "Kazmer, I have a job for you. I want you to work with Travers and get me more videos. Do whatever is necessary. I want to see this contract play out. I'm not sure how you would orchestrate this, but I trust the two of you to figure it out. Use Radford if need be."

Just then, a tall, thin man entered the office. He was Jonas Radford, the other person who rounded out Carmotte's inner circle. His journey to that coveted position had taken much longer than Kazmer's.

Radford had always been someone Travers could count on to deliver whatever he was asked. He did exactly what he was told and well, but that was exactly where he fell short. Much like Kazmer, Radford was an adept assassin. But what had held him back over the years was his lack of leadership skills. Kazmer had no problem managing others. In fact, he was pretty comfortable both taking the lead and falling in line under someone else. Nonetheless, all three men seemed to complement one another, creating a solid wall Carmotte could remain comfortably inside of.

Radford held two large paper bags with grease spots on the outside. From the bags, he pulled out double bacon cheeseburgers and sacks of fries.

"Perfect timing, Radford. Eating this burger while watching the video is the perfect pairing. Did you get the vanilla milkshakes?"

Radford nodded. From the other bag, he plucked out three shakes.

"Mmm, I just can't get enough of these shakes," Carmotte said. "The vanilla flavor is so pure. Have any of you heard from Travers?"

"I spoke with him this morning. He's heading to New York," Kazmer said. "He thinks that's where Sei is eventually heading."

"What's in New York? Oh, wait. I think I know. Travers thinks she's going to meet Willie. You know what happened the last time in New York, right? Travers failed miserably there. In fact, he's been failing a lot lately."

"He's done exceptionally well on overseeing the contract," Radford said, doing his best to defend the man who wasn't there to protect himself.

"He has. Travers is my most trusted man and has been with me since the beginning. I should cut him some slack, but I just don't have the patience. I want you both to keep an eye on Travers in case he slips and needs a little help."

The men nodded.

24

After finishing their burgers and fries, Kazmer and Radford left Carmotte alone to obsess over the video.

"What do you think?" Radford asked as they walked down a hall toward an elevator.

Ever since being paired up with Kazmer on a previous job, Radford often sought Kazmer's opinion. He trusted the quiet man's advice and, above all else, admired his ability to remain completely neutral in every situation—the consummate diplomat. It wasn't an easy line to straddle. Both men reported to Travers but also couldn't ignore Carmotte, as he was the head honcho. They often found themselves caught in the middle, having to juggle the egos of both men. Radford had quickly grown comfortable with following Kazmer's lead.

"If we offer Travers help, he'll get defensive," Radford said, pushing the call button. "He's already insecure about his position with Carmotte. The last thing we need is to lose his trust and have him turn against us."

"I think that's exactly what Carmotte wants," Kazmer replied. "He wants to see if he can still count on Travers to be his number two."

"You think Travers is on the way out?"

The two men stepped into the elevator.

"No, I think his position is secure, but any further screw-ups and Carmotte won't hesitate to end their relationship."

"What? They've been together like twenty years?"

"Something like that."

"Part of me thinks being a gun for hire is easier, less stressful. I don't do well with politics."

The elevator doors opened, and they stepped out two floors lower. The private suite occupied five entire floors. They walked past leather couches and across a floor covered in intricate oriental rugs. The floor-to-ceiling windows gave enticing views of the city.

"Do you really think Carmotte will let you go after all you've been exposed to in his organization?" Kazmer asked. "Think about his reach."

"Are you saying we're trapped here?" Radford walked around behind a bar and retrieved two bottles of Pellegrino from the refrigerator, then placed them on the bar.

Kazmer took a seat on a barstool and twisted the cap off one of the bottles. "What I'm saying is we work for the devil. And he doesn't accept resignations."

Radford shook his head in disappointment. "So, what do we do?"

Kazmer took a long swig before answering. "We do exactly as he says."

"Travers will go apeshit when we tell him."

"And that's why we won't tell him. Carmotte said to keep an eye on him. He didn't say to interfere. So that's what we'll do."

Radford took a sip from his bottle as his gaze settled on the view from the forty-fifth floor.

"We should take the first flight to New York," Kazmer said.

"What about Carmotte? Travers was very clear when he said

not to leave him alone. He believes him to be unstable at the moment."

"We have no choice. Carmotte's wishes overrule Travers."

Radford took another sip from his bottle. "How familiar are you with Willie?"

"Not very much. I only know of him."

"Same here. But if anyone can find Carmotte, it's him. Why don't we just take him out? Without Willie, Sei is back to square one. Of course, if we do that, Travers will figure out we did it. He'll likely turn on us, and we'll be caught in a war between him and Carmotte, one where we're likely to be a casualty."

"He sees Willie as bait and is willing to wager he'll get to Sei before Willie can find Carmotte. Killing Willie isn't an option for us," Kazmer said.

"So, what do you propose?"

"We do as Carmotte asked. We keep an eye on Travers."

25

I t took longer to reach Richmond than I had anticipated. I arrived just before sunrise, so I resolved to find a motel and sleep during the day. I could make the final push to New York as soon as the night came again.

When I woke, I found myself in the exact same position as when I had first laid down. The time was a little after four-thirty. I was a bit surprised that I'd slept the entire day without any disturbance. I climbed out of bed and peeked through the blackout curtains. I still had a few hours to kill before it got dark enough for me to get back on the road.

I grabbed my cell phone, navigated to the private chat room that Willie and I used, and found that he'd answered me just an hour ago. I quickly typed out a reply.

Sei: You'll be in my sights soon.

I waited, hoping he'd stuck around. A few seconds later, he replied.

Willie: It's not safe.

One minute later, my cell phone rang. A number I didn't recognize appeared on the screen. *Willie?* I answered but said nothing. That was the protocol. Willie would answer first with the correct word.

"Basketball," a voice said on the other end.

"Woo Woo," I said. "Willie, why are you calling and not using the chat room?"

"It's been compromised. Someone hacked into it."

"How?"

"I'm not sure, but it can only be one person behind it."

"Wait, does Ethan know it's us in the room?"

"I don't think so. We didn't say much, and our identities were masked. I think it's a bot that's crawling through chat rooms on the dark web. But we shouldn't use it. We can speak freely now, but not for long."

"I'm in Richmond. I'll be in New York later tonight. Have you learned anything?"

"I don't have good news, Sei. I haven't been able to locate Ethan. It'll be difficult if he's not accessing the web or has others taking orders from him."

"When I last encountered him, he was surrounded by three men. I think we should focus on them. One is named Bradford Travers, and the other goes by Kazmer. He's an assassin. The third I don't know, but I know what he looks like."

"Finding more information on these men *can* lead to finding Ethan," Willie said. "It'll take longer."

"Right now, they are protecting him. If I can pick them off, it'll expose Ethan."

"I'll await your arrival."

Willie disconnected the call. We wouldn't speak again until I arrived in New York. Even though Willie would now focus on the two names I'd given him, that didn't mean I couldn't get started.

Kazmer was involved in my daughter's kidnapping, and Mui had interacted with him during that time. I never really pushed her to tell me more about him, as I had become so focused on Ethan. But in light of the current situation, I might need to contact Mui—something I'd avoided doing ever since the contract had been issued for me.

I removed the SIM card from the phone I had just used and broke it before retrieving another SIM card from my backpack. I dialed her cell phone. The call connected, and someone picked up on the other end. I didn't expect her to say anything. She wasn't supposed to.

"Mui, it's me," I said.

"Mother! Oh my God, I'm so happy to hear from you. I've been so worried. How are you? Where are you? When can I see you?"

"Mui, the situation is still the same."

"Oh," she said, deflated. "I understand."

"I'm sorry. I want you to know I'm okay and safe. How are you?"

"I'm fine. Everything is great here."

"I'm glad to hear that. Are things well with Ryan?"

Ryan Yee was Mui's boyfriend, and the teenage son of Abby Kane. Abby and I had a weird relationship, given the sides of the law we both lived on, but there was mutual respect and trust between us. Plus, our kids were dating and had been for over three years. Those were reasons that helped me to ask for Abby's help. There was no one else I could entrust with my daughter's safety.

"He's fine. Really, Ryan's family has been nothing but supportive toward me. I'm homeschooling and doing well, but I miss my friends. Really, I miss you the most."

"And I miss you, too. I need to know more about Kazmer. Tell me everything as quickly as you can."

Mui spent the next twenty minutes recapping what she could remember about Kazmer, everything from a physical description to his personality to even the conversations they'd had. She'd met Travers only briefly; same for the third man, but she never learned his name. Worried about being on the call too long, I ended it quickly and told her that I loved her.

I grabbed a water bottle off the bedside table and finished it off before looking over the equipment I had picked up from Ivan. Inside the duffel bag next to my bed was enough ammunition for two new handguns: Glock 19s. I had suppressors for each one. I also had ten throwing knives, a garrote, two palm knives, and a sheathed hunting knife. I also had a small Sig P365 that was perfect for an ankle holster. I was satisfied with what I had.

During my call with Mui, my stomach grumbled. My last proper meal before I checked into the motel was a while ago. I peeked out through the curtains and watched a family load their belongings into an SUV. Parked across the road was a food truck selling tacos. I kept watch, waiting for a break in the flow of customers. When the last person walked away with their food, I put on my jacket, pulled my ball cap low across my head, and slipped on dark sunglasses. I took a palm knife from the bag and left my room.

I scanned the menu at the taco truck briefly while an elderly Hispanic woman waited to take my order. It looked like her husband operated the grill.

"Number two taco combo, please," I said. "And a bottle of water."

"What filling do you want?" she asked.

"Carnitas."

The lady nodded. "Six dollars."

I handed over the money and stepped off to the side while I waited. The family in the SUV pulled out of the motel parking lot and drove away. A minute later, a pickup truck pulled off the road and parked ahead of the taco truck. Two white men exited the pickup and looked at me. I casually placed a hand into my jacket pocket and gripped the palm knife. They eyed me until they reached the truck.

Just then, the lady called out, "Two taco combo."

I took the brown paper bag from her and left.

"Nice ass," I heard one of the men say. For a second, I thought of addressing him but decided he wasn't worth the breath.

I crossed the road and headed back to my room on the second floor of the building. Before entering my room, I glanced back and saw that both were watching me.

Scavies?

I didn't think I was recognizable with the hat and sunglasses, but I had to consider it. The video of me fighting Iron Wolf would not have gone unnoticed. The bullseye on my back had doubled in size.

I closed the door behind me and peeked outside the curtain. I watched them until they got their food and drove off. Only then did I sit down and eat. I still looked outside every few minutes.

After eating, I took a quick shower and then got ready to leave. I slipped on a double shoulder holster that was capable of holding both handguns. I also had a custom-made utility belt that I had obtained from an arms dealer who worked out of Jamaica Hills, New York. It could hold six throwing knives, extra magazines, a garrote, and a palm knife. If need be, I was confident I could visit this dealer and restock.

When night came, I put the rest of my belongings into my backpack, put my helmet on, and left my room. As I made my way down the stairs, I caught sight of the pickup truck I'd seen earlier. Through the windshield, I could see the outlines of two men.

Dumb move.

I had to make a decision. Were they scavies or idiots? I couldn't take the chance. I walked over to the truck and knocked on the driver's side window, tinted dark. The window rolled down, revealing two men smiling at me.

"What do you want?" I asked.

"Just want to know if you want to hang out and party," the driver said.

"You think sitting in the parking lot and stalking me is the best way to ask me out?"

The man laughed as he looked over at his friend in the passenger seat.

"Aw, come on now. We're all friends here. How about you lift up that visor so we can get a good look at your face. You know what they say about what makes a woman hot. Distance. We need to confirm." He laughed again.

"Trust me, you're nowhere near my league," I said.

"Hey now, you don't have to be a bitch. We just wanted to have fun," the driver said. He looked over at his friend. "This bitch thinks she's something." He shifted in his seat as he removed something from the center console. He raised his hand just enough so I could see his handgun. "I'm going to ask your bitch ass one more time, do you—"

I punched my palm knife into the side of his neck and unleashed a red torrent. Before the passenger could react, I reached across and did the same to him. Both men were gagging as they held their hands tightly around their necks. It was pointless. They were already dead. I opened the door, raised the window back up, and shut it before heading to my motorcycle. I just couldn't take chances with any encounter I had.

26

I nterstate 95 runs from Florida to the Canada–United States border in Maine. It was an easy straight shot north from Richmond, especially on a Wednesday night. Traffic wasn't heavy, and I reached New York a little before midnight. A wave of relief rushed over my body as I could focus entirely on locating Ethan and ending the contract.

Willie owned a four-story building in New York's Chinatown on Doyers Street. It was off the tourist path—only locals ever frequented that part of Chinatown. He'd been in this exact location for as long as I'd known him. On the second floor, he operated a tiny cybercafé that also doubled as a printer shop—his cover. He would often change the name of his business. The last time I'd visited, his shop was called Supreme Cyber & Printing Café. Because he rarely left his place and rarely met with anyone there, very few people knew he resided in Chinatown.

At that time of night, the shops on Doyers would all be closed, and foot traffic would be nil. Next door was a Chinese herb specialist, and occupying the ground space of his building was a dim sum restaurant. If my memory served me correctly, it was called Dee Dee's Dim Sum. Willie didn't have a storefront, only a tinted glass door with a tiny sign signaled the existence of the café.

As I drove past his location, I noticed he'd changed the shop's name to Excellent Cyber & Print Café. The restaurant had diners inside. It was New York; people were always eating at all hours. I looped around the block and parked my bike not far from Willie's business. As I approached, the smell of food from the restaurant awakened my hunger. I stopped inside and got an order of dumplings and char siu bao. Willie would appreciate it.

I pushed on the glass door and was surprised to find it unlocked. I thought for sure I'd have to message him to let me in. I locked the door and flipped the open sign to closed. Directly inside was a narrow staircase that creaked with every step. The lights in the stairway were off, but once I reached the landing, I could see the light shining through the edges of a closed door ahead. I continued through and entered a small, cluttered area.

It looked exactly as I remembered from my last visit. The small countertop with a tiny silver bell was unmanned. Boxes of printing paper were stacked against the walls. A letterboard menu listed printing services. The neon sign that read Cyber had been turned off. I knew from the security camera above the counter and the one in the stairway that Willie was already aware I had arrived. I tapped the bell on the counter and waited. A few seconds later, an elderly man appeared from behind a curtained doorway.

"Sei," Willie said as a smile formed on his face.

He walked hunched with a cane for support and still had his trademark wispy beard. He was dressed in a red and black Tang suit made from silk. His hair was a mixture of salt and pepper, and the sunspots I remembered on his cheeks were still there.

His real name was Wayne Wong. Willie was a nickname derived from a famous Chinese basketball player: Willie "Woo Woo" Wong.

"I've brought food," I said as I gave him a gentle hug.

"And I've just prepared a pot of tea. Come with me. We have much to discuss," he said before leading me through the curtained doorway.

I'd first met Willie years ago when I was still actively working as an assassin. The job required me to navigate through numerous Chinatowns worldwide, and he'd helped me maintain contact with my employer.

"Please have a seat." He pointed to a round antique table made from teakwood with mother-of-pearl inlay. There were five matching chairs.

"Let me help you," I offered as I watched him pick up a tray holding a teapot and cups.

"I'm fine. Please take a seat, Sei."

He placed the tray on the table. I poured the tea while he fetched two plates and chopsticks.

"Here's to our health and prosperity," he said, holding up his cup before taking a sip. "How was your journey, Sei?"

Over tea and dim sum, I told Willie everything that had happened since I'd left San Francisco. He was content to listen with the occasional nod. Only when I'd finished did he ask his first question.

"How is Mui?"

"She's fine. Thank you for asking. I spoke with her briefly while I was in Richmond."

"I hope I have a chance to meet her one day. Sei, do you have other plans while you're here in New York?"

"I need to visit a contact here. He has access to supplies. What I have now is sufficient, but I'd like to see what he has on offer."

"Can you trust this person?"

"I believe I can. Outside of that, I have no other plans than to work alongside you in finding Ethan."

It had been discussed earlier that I would stay with Willie. He would need my protection during this time.

"Now it's time for me to speak." Willie leaned forward, resting his forearms on the table. "There is not much to tell you regarding Ethan. I am having trouble finding any information on his whereabouts. I know you thought all you needed to do was make it to New York alive and everything would fall into place."

"Yes, that's exactly what I thought."

"If I can be frank with my words..." He paused.

I nodded.

"I don't think dissolving the contract will be easy, nor do I think it will happen fast. It will take time. You will be attacked more times than you can imagine before you can end this."

"The longer the contract is live, the greater the odds of someone... I can't win them all."

"I know, Sei. But you have no choice. You must find a way to fend off every attack. You must accept that this will be your life for however long it takes."

Willie's words were a wake-up call. I had wanted to believe from the very start that all I needed to do was find and kill Ethan and it would be over. Mui and I would be able to resume our happy lives together. But all I did was convince myself that this was simply another problem to deal with just like all the others in the past. The reality? I might not be able to fix this mess.

"Keep your spirits up, Sei. I have learned more about two of the other names you mentioned to me."

Willie told me everything he learned about Kazmer. Most of it was information my daughter had conveyed to me previously, but hearing it from Willie provided confirmation.

"Kazmer is Hungarian. From what I've learned, he doesn't accept very many jobs. He's picky about his employers and is quick to move on if they don't suit his taste."

"Mui first encountered him two years ago," I said. "That would suggest that he and Ethan have struck a deal."

"It would, and it explains why you saw them together."

"He must have proven himself worthy to Ethan during his first job. I know Ethan's style of management is very hands-off. When we were dating, there was another man who did most of his bidding. I never met him in person, but he represented Ethan in all of his business dealings."

"That man is Bradford Travers. And you are right. He is the person who has represented Ethan in business. This is why Ethan's identity was kept hidden for so long. I also learned Travers was responsible for hiring Vegas, the assassin who attacked you the last time you were here in New York. I've secured a photo of him just to double-check."

Willie produced a printed photograph of a man. "Is this one of the men you saw surrounding Ethan?"

"Yes, it is."

"This is Ethan's second-in-command. Eliminate him, and you will start to cripple Ethan, maybe even stop the dossier from updating."

"You know about that?"

He nodded. "Yes. And it just recently has been updated. Did you leave two bodies in Richmond?"

"I did."

"It's listed here. It's not confirmed, but it is suggested that you were responsible and could be in that area. Sei, anything that could be attributed to you is being logged here." Willie's brow crinkled. "It's vital you don't attract attention. Right now, you are your own biggest enemy."

"Willie, if anything that might be attributed to me could be listed on here, I can use that as a strategic advantage by giving them the impression that I'm in places I am not."

"If you can do that, you will be able to stay one step ahead."

27

Willie and I talked well into the early morning hours, until 3:00 a.m. I instructed Willie not to leave the front door unlocked. I also told him I would arrange for a proper door, not a glass one—at least until I no longer needed his help, and I felt his safety was secured. I suggested he close his shop and offered to cover any revenue loss, which I doubted was much. Willie made his money from selling information. He said he'd consider it.

The following day I woke later than usual, at 9:00 a.m. On the third floor of Willie's building, directly above his shop with it's small living room, bathroom, and kitchen, was a sitting area and a bedroom, where I stayed. The top floor was Willie's bedroom. It was an open plan (no doors), so all I did was head up and peek inside. He was sleeping soundly in his bed.

I headed down to the second floor and put a kettle on the stove before checking the building entrance. The door was still secured, but it wouldn't take much to break through the glass. I peeked outside. Chinatown was already up, and its residents were bustling up and down the sidewalks. Shops were open, and the bakery across the street was packed with locals.

My priority for the day was to bolster my supplies. I had to accept that Travers would find me and send everyone he could to take me down. Willie's building wasn't the most secure location, but I had been confident I could defend it with a capable arsenal. But a thorough walk-through showed me the building was in much worse shape than I had thought. Infiltration would be a walk in the park for just about anyone. No need to leave a welcome mat out inviting people in.

I made a list of all the vulnerable entry points: the front door, the rooftop, and the windows. Reinforcing all entry points and placing security cameras on the outside of the building would go a long way toward securing the property, especially the roof.

The access door was flimsy and needed to be replaced. There was no space between the buildings, so one could walk across the rooftops of every building by just climbing over a foot-tall parapet. Across the street, the buildings were mostly the same height, but a few were a floor taller. A sniper could easily nest in any one of those windows and see into Willie's building. A lot of work needed to be done, fast.

I headed back down to the second floor from the roof and called Dorothy Black. She was the assistant headmaster at Confrere Preparatory Academy, the school my daughter used to attend in the Bay Area. She had a relationship with an arms dealer in New York. Why does the assistant headmaster at a private school have a relationship with an arms dealer? Let's just say she works in the same profession I've been trying to retire from. It was still early on the West Coast, but I thought I'd take a chance.

"Dorothy Black's office. How may I help you?"

"Lottie, it's Sei."

Lottie Kingsley was her trusted assistant.

"Well, this is an unexpected call," she said.

"I'm glad you're in the office."

"Actually, I'm not. I forgot that I had the calls forwarded. I'm at my place."

"I'm sorry to disturb you so early, but I need to speak to Dorothy. It's rather urgent. Is there a way for you to put me in touch with her?"

"I'm afraid not. Is there something I can help you with?"

"I believe you can. I need to meet with Dorothy's contact here in New York as soon as possible. You know who I'm talking about, right?"

"Yes, of course. I'll work on arranging a meeting. I'll call you back on this number as soon as I have something finalized."

I disconnected the call. While I waited, I reheated the kettle and poured myself a cup of tea. Willie appeared a few minutes later.

"Good morning, Sei. How did you sleep?" he asked.

"Fine, thank you." I poured Willie a cup of tea.

"Good, good. I was worried the bed would be too stiff for you."

"It wasn't."

Just then, my phone rang.

"Hello, Sei. It's Lottie calling. I've secured a meeting for you. He is waiting, and you can head over."

"Thank you for your help."

"Business?" Willie asked.

"Yes. I'll need to step away for a few hours."

"I'll be fine here. I've always been fine here."

"Willie, this morning I inspected your building. We'll need to reinforce entry points and set up a security system."

A frown appeared on his face. "Do you think that's really necessary? Everyone here knows me. This is my home."

"I realize that, but the residents of Chinatown are not the ones we need to watch out for. We must get started as soon as possible. My arms contact should be able to help. I promise when all of this is over, we can change everything back to how it was."

"It's fine, Sei. Do what you need to do."

"I made oxtail and bean stew. You will love it over coconut rice," Jalissa said.

Jackson fixed me a bowl of rice and stew and placed it down in front of me.

"Go on, Sei," he said. "You'll see that the meat is tender and falls right off the bone."

With all eyes on me, how could I resist? I used my spoon to cut through a piece of meat like it was warm butter. I scooped up rice, beans, and the gravy and took it all into my mouth at once. The thick stew was flavorful, and I definitely tasted the allspice.

"This is wonderful, Jalissa," I said after swallowing a bite. "I've never tried oxtail before."

We spent the next hour eating and telling stories. Mostly it was Jackson and his wife relaying tales of the past and updating me on the present; currently, their oldest daughter was entering high school as a freshman. I think they knew it made no sense for me to tell any stories. My situation was not a secret, but hearing their positive and loving stories made me feel better. It gave me hope that I would one day settle back down.

After we finished our meal, Jackson and I excused ourselves to discuss business. Meetings took place in his basement, never, ever in front of his wife or children.

A steel door secured Jackson's basement. It had a fingerprint access pad. Cages lined the walls inside the room. That was where he locked up his inventory. In the center of the room was the metal table he used to lay out his customer's selections.

He rested his hands on his waist. "Sei, tell me what you're hoping to accomplish with additional weapons."

"I'm not sure what I'll need. This isn't a job that I'm preparing for. It's defense. I don't want to be caught off guard. I have handguns, ammo, and throwing knives, but that's it. I do still have the custom utility belt I got from you the last time."

He smiled broadly. "I'm very proud of it. I'm assuming you

have nothing left of what I supplied you with during your last visit?"

"That's correct."

He clapped his hands. "Okay, let's get to work."

Jackson began removing items from the cages and placing them on the table. I was familiar with most of what he had selected, but I remained quiet and let him do his job.

"These are basics needed for any situation." He retrieved a sniper rifle from one of the cages. "This is completely different from the rifle I supplied the last time. This is a Sig Cross Rifle. It's lightweight, only six and a half pounds. Perfect for urban warfare. You can easily whip it out in an instant, fire, and then tuck it away and be on the move again. It has an upgraded, ten-round magazine and comes with a bipod if you need steadiness The optics work well at night. The skeletonized folding stock makes it easy to carry around in a bag. The range is about six hundred yards. It's extremely versatile, which you will need. It's bolt action, so keep that in mind if you have multiple targets moving in on your position."

I took the rifle from Jackson and examined it.

"Have you fired this rifle before?" he asked.

"Once, but it was years ago. I liked it."

"I'm also recommending the Sig Rattler, easily the most compact assault rifle on the market. It's perfect for extreme close-quarters combat. Nothing better for tight spots. It also has a foldable stock. It can be outfitted with a suppressor, but that will lengthen it, though not by much. The mag capacity is thirty rounds. Versatility, Sei."

"I liked the titanium throwing knives you supplied the last time. I'll need more."

"No problem. What about a tactical shotgun? It can double as a doorbell."

"These two rifles will do just fine. I need a security expert who can secure an old building: cameras, tripwires, silent alarms, reinforced doors and windows. I need it all. Right now, a child could infiltrate the place I'm staying at. Can you help with that?"

"I can't, but my cousin Sanka can. He is the best."

Jackson made a quick call.

"It's done," he announced, disconnecting. "He's on his way over here now. He can return with you and look over the property, make recommendations and then get to work. He has a trusted team that can work quickly under any conditions."

"Perfect."

While Jackson gathered my gear together and placed it into a duffel bag, I transferred funds into his account.

"I'm throwing in extra ammo, Sei. You can never have too much. And you might not have an opportunity to acquire more. Also, two tactical medical kits because you never know."

"Thank you, Lamont. You've been extremely accommodating."

"If you leave the country, you may now contact me directly. I have trusted partners around the world who can help you re-up your supply." He plugged his secure number into my phone.

We headed back upstairs and had a long goodbye with Jalissa while waiting for Jackson's cousin to arrive.

Fifteen minutes passed before a black SUV came to a stop at the curb in front of Jackson's home.

"Sanka!" Jackson called out from the porch.

"Lamont. Long time, my friend," said a man who matched Jackson's energy.

"Sanka, I want you to meet Sei. She's a terrific woman."

"It's nice to meet you, Ms. Sei."

"Likewise. You can call me Sei."

"She's on a tight schedule," Jackson said. "It's best you guys get going."

"Yes, of course. You can brief us when we reach the location," Sanka said. "Will you be riding with us?"

"That's my bike over there." I pointed. "You can follow me."

"Okay, okay. Let me take your gear. It'll be easier." He took the duffel bag from me. "Where are we going?"

"Chinatown."

29

W hen we arrived in Chinatown, I asked Sanka and his men to wait outside. I wanted to brief Willie before letting these men into his place. He wasn't a fan of strangers.

"Sei, I don't know these men, and you want to invite them inside," Willie said as he sipped his tea. "That's not how things work."

"I realize that, but under the circumstances, I believe it's necessary. We need to secure the building. These men come highly recommended from a trusted contact."

After a bit more back and forth, Willie agreed to let the team enter. I made a quick introduction before walking Sanka and his men through the premises.

Sanka's recommendations started with replacing the entire front door, as I had already suspected, in addition to reinforcing the windows.

"I have a man in New York who can deliver a door. I can modify it to have a security pad that requires a keycard, fingerprint, eyeball...it's up to you. Also, we need to wire the door and windows with sensors. Anyone trying to enter will trip a silent alarm. We'll place cameras in and outside the building. I also recommend placing cameras on the building directly across the road and at either end of the street. Let me worry about how that gets done."

"How will I control all of this?" I asked, a bit worried he'd want to install a command center in Willie's place.

"You will be able to control everything from a smartphone. If an alarm is tripped, you'll know. You'll be able to cycle through all of the cameras. You don't need to be on the property."

We headed up to the roof, where my biggest concern lay.

"This is problematic, Sei," Sanka said. "Having sensors up here will notify you, but it won't stop anyone from crossing over from the building next door. We'll reinforce the door, and that'll slow them, but if they want to get in, C-4 will do the trick."

"What about snipers from the building across the road?"

"If I install ballistic glass, it'll stop handguns easily but not a high-powered rifle—especially if someone fires a 50 caliber. My advice would be to replace the windows that are most vulnerable with steel. Even thermal imaging won't work then. Nothing to see, nothing to shoot at. The rest of the windows can be outfitted with ballistic glass."

"How long will it take to do all of this?" I asked.

"Two full days. But I want to warn you now: It's impossible to make this place one hundred percent secure. If someone wants to get in, they will get in. But you'll at least have a heads up and can prepare."

I gave Sanka the okay to move forward. I wanted to make it as hard as possible for anyone who actually figured out where I was to get to me. The precautions mainly were for Willie's sake. I knew I could defend myself, but I couldn't be sure I could protect Willie from whatever unknown threats arose. And I was the reason why any harm could come to him.

I joined Willie on the second floor, and he poured me a cup of tea.

"Are they starting?" he asked.

"Yes. And again, I assure you we can get rid of all this stuff later."

"I understand why you're doing this, Sei. It's for my protection. I'm not stupid. I know helping you endangers me. I'm aware of that, but I still want to help you. Do you have other engagements to attend to today?"

"I do not. Let's get to work."

THE PEGASUS MOTOR home was cruising along I-80, just outside of Hackensack, New Jersey. Travers sat in the front passenger seat. He was staring at his phone when Gary inquired about the plan.

"Should I head straight into Manhattan, to the place in the East Village?"

"No, it's been compromised," Travers answered.

"That's a shame. I liked that building. Do you have another location in mind?"

"I've been unable to secure another safe house."

"I see."

Travers was in a foul mood. He blamed Gary for the late arrival to the city. He'd been unable to make the drive to New York without rest. Travers didn't want to drive, nor did he trust Rocha or Tran to drive the million-dollar motor home, so they arrived later than Travers had wished to. It didn't bother Gary. Travers was acting like a big baby, and he was used to it.

"Shall I just drive around the city?"

Travers let out a loud breath as he dramatically lowered his phone. "Sheesh, Gary, do I need to make every single decision?"

"No, I'm happy to make them all from here on out. Feel free to take a nap. I'll wake you in a few days."

Travers shot Gary a look. "I'm hungry. Go to that deli that I like."

"I can do that."

Forty-five minutes later, Gary brought the motor home to stop near Second Avenue and East Third Street. New York's Best Deli, aptly named, was located at that corner.

"Do you want me to head in and pick up the usual?" Gary asked.

"No, I need to stretch my legs," Travers responded.

Travers exited Pegasus and headed inside. It was coming up on lunch, so the deli had a decent crowd of people placing orders at the counter. Travers stood in line patiently. He already knew what he wanted: a corned beef sandwich and steak fries. When he reached the counter, he spotted a familiar face behind the register.

"My friend," the young man said upon seeing Travers. "How are you? Will you be having the corned beef sandwich with fries?"

"Yes, but make it four orders."

"My friend, where have you been? It's been so long since I've seen you."

"I've been busy."

"Out of town?"

"Never mind where."

"No problem. I'm just happy to see you again."

"Are you still in school?" Travers asked.

"Yes, I am. It's my final year. I'm so excited."

"Don't be. The world is a cruel place."

The young man laughed hesitantly. "Sure, of course. Is there anything else I can get for you?"

"A couple of containers of potato salad and a bunch of your whole dill pickles."

"No problem."

Travers paid for his order and then waited off to the side. About fifteen minutes later, the young man behind the counter handed him two large bags.

"Enjoy, my friend. See you soon."

Travers nodded and left the deli. Back inside the motor home, he passed out sandwiches and fries.

"There's potato salad and pickles in the bag," he said.

"Don't mind if I do. You know I love their potato salad," Gary said.

"What the hell kind of food is this?" Tran said, holding up a sandwich that was the size of his face.

"Shut up and eat it, kid," Travers said.

"So you never answered my question about why you're so sure Sei came to New York," Gary said before taking a bite of his sandwich.

"I hired someone to come after her the last time she was in New York."

"Did that person find her?"

"He did, but sadly he wasn't up to the task of finishing the job."

Travers showed Gary the uploaded footage of a deadly assassin in a stairwell.

"His name is Vegas. I thought he had the skills to take her out. As you can see, I gave him too much credit."

"Where is this?"

"I don't know. I just know Vegas had tracked her down and had been waiting for an opportunity to strike."

"You know what you should do? Upload that footage to the dossier. Tell everyone Sei is somewhere in New York. Identify this stairwell, and they'll find her."

30

That same afternoon, Kazmer and Radford's flight touched down at JFK International Airport. The two men quickly made their way through immigration, collected their luggage, and met with the driver hired to take them into the city.

Once settled in the backseat of the silver Town Car, Radford turned to Kazmer. "Any thoughts yet on the best way to keep an eye on Travers without him knowing?"

"Not exactly. But let's focus on the positive. He's in New York, and he's driving around in a large black motor home. It shouldn't be hard to find him. We'll play it by ear."

"It's a shame the safe house in the city was compromised."

"Is it? As far as I know, Carmotte still owns the building."

"You're not actually thinking of staying there, are you? Is it even furnished?"

"Worth a look. If not, we'll stay in a hotel room."

"I'm always a little confused as to what Carmotte wants, but you seem to have a good handle on reading between the lines. What is he really asking us to do here?"

"He still thinks Travers is under delivering."

Radford shifted in his seat. "Yeah, I'm not vouching for his performance with kidnapping that girl. What was her name again?"

"Mui."

"Yeah, that's it. Anyway, I thought he'd redeemed himself with the contract. I mean, that livestream was golden, even if he wasn't completely responsible."

"I agree, but we work for a psychopath. Carmotte remembers what he wants. And because that's the way it is, it becomes his reality. Let that be a reminder."

No SOONER HAD Travers left the deli than the young man behind the register stepped away from the counter to make a phone call.

"Dorothy Black's office. How may I help you?"

"Hello, Ms. Kingsley?"

"Yes, this is she. And whom am I speaking with?"

"This is Mohamed Abadi from the deli in New York. Do you remember?"

"Yes, of course, Mohamed. What a pleasant surprise. How did you get a hold of this number?"

"Google."

"I see. Well, how may I help you?"

"I'm calling because I've seen him again, the man who comes into my deli and orders corned beef sandwiches."

"You mean Kazmer?" Ms. Kingsley asked.

"No, the other one. I don't know his name. I only call him 'my friend.'"

There was brief pause. "And why might you believe it to be important to me?"

"Uh, I dunno. I just know it was really important last time. I thought you'd want to know."

"I see. This wouldn't have anything to do with a finder's fee, now would it?"

"If you feel my actions merit it, I wouldn't be opposed to accepting one," Mohamed said politely.

"I understand. What other information can you provide about him?"

"Instead of ordering two sandwiches like he normally does, he ordered four. He's never ordered that much. He has friends with him."

"Or he's unusually hungry," Kingsley offered.

"No, I've seen them. I looked outside when he left. He got into a large motor home. It's too big for one person."

"Anything else?"

"He said he had been busy, and I asked if he had been out of town. I stopped asking questions because he started to get irritated."

"Can I reach you at this number?"

"Yes, it's my cell phone."

"Thank you for calling. I'll be in touch."

Abadi pocketed his phone and peeked outside the deli once more. The black motorhome was still there, so he discreetly snapped a couple of pictures with his phone.

This should be worth a finder's fee.

THE TOWN CAR pulled up alongside the building that Travers and Carmotte would periodically stay while in the city. The shades were drawn across the windows and the front door had a lockbox attached to the doorknob.

"Wait for us," Kazmer told the driver.

He and Radford climbed out of the car and made their way to the door.

"Do you know the combination to the lockbox?" Radford asked as he eyed the device.

"Nope."

Kazmer removed a pair of leather gloves from his jacket and slipped them on before punching through the thin glass of one of the windows. He cleared away the broken bits and they climbed inside.

"I heard a cleaning crew had to come through here and removed a couple of bodies," Radford said as they hit the landing of the second floor. "Do you know what happened?"

"Travers left two men here in case Sei and her friends figured out where the safe house was. Remember the other woman who appeared on the cargo ship?"

"Yeah,"

"Apparently, she was the one who disposed of them."

"Why didn't Carmotte put a contract out on her? She killed a lot of his men."

"Carmotte doesn't care about the hired help. He wants Sei because of their past."

"You seem to know a lot about Carmotte."

"Keep your eyes and ears open, and you will too."

They continued to explore the building. On the top floor, Kazmer pointed to a door at the end of the hall.

"That was Carmotte's office. It's where I first met him."

Radford scanned the area and shrugged. "This place is totally empty. Not much use unless we need a location where we have to hold someone for an indefinite amount of time."

31

Willie wanted time alone while he worked, so I took the opportunity to pick up some personal items and extra clothing. It had been a while since I had gotten a proper workout in, and I was craving it.

I headed over to the gym near Spring Street and Lafayette Street in Tribeca with a new athletic outfit and purchased a one-day pass. The place was small and hardcore—not one of those large chain gyms that catered to trends and influencers. I changed into my workout clothes, stuck my backpack into a locker, and hit the floor.

After twenty minutes, I spent time with the heavy bag. It felt great to get my aggression out with every punch. It also helped me think through my situation and how I'd changed my strategy from Carmotte to focus on his inner circle. I couldn't help but feel like I'd started all over again from scratch. At least I knew what those men looked like.

Surely there was a hierarchy amongst them. It made me wonder if I should focus on one of them or just go after whoever was available. I knew the most about Kazmer, only because Mui had interacted with him a lot during her abduction. Did I need to focus on him? I wasn't sure at the moment. What I wanted was to see all of them dead.

"Nice form," a voice said, pulling me out of my thoughts.

The man stood off to the side. He looked like any person who came to the gym. It was a weekday, so I assumed he was jobless, worked shifts, or was self-employed.

"What's that?" I asked, even though I'd heard him the first time.

"I said you have nice form."

During the initial few seconds of our conversation, I had determined his interest in me wasn't because of the contract. Assassins normally don't spend time making small talk with their targets. Could he have been a scavie? Doubtful. The big grin wasn't convincing. That left one explanation: He was hitting on me.

"Thank you."

"Do you need me to hold the bag while you continue?"

"That won't be necessary."

"My name is Sid Quinn." He held out his hand as he continued to smile.

"Nice to meet you, Sid. If you don't mind, I'd like to continue my workout."

He held both hands up in front of him. "Sure, no problem. Enjoy."

As I watched him walk away, I realized it had been a while since I'd had any contact with someone who was genuine about their interests with me. The idea of having people in my life had always been foreign to me because of my profession. Aside from my daughter, only a handful of other people had been successful in breaking down my walls. The first was Kostas Demos, a man I had met while searching for my daughter the first time she'd been taking from me. He had been with me throughout that journey, providing support and guidance, especially during the times I felt like giving up. He also played a significant role in helping locate her. Sadly, he lost his life while helping me.

The second group of people I had grown close to was the staff hired to work for me. After I rescued Mui from the Black Wolf, I needed to set up new identities for us—my past would always bring trouble. I decided to settle in Greece, Nafplio, to be exact, and took Kostas' last name as our own in his memory. It was in Nafplio that I owned and operated a boutique hotel named Opa!

Living in Greece allowed me to open up in ways I never thought possible. A large part of that was my ability to be a mother to Mui. Also, the hotel staff had become a second family to us. I trusted them, and they were loyal to us. Life was good in the seaport town. That is, until Ethan came back into the picture.

I couldn't risk putting the people closest to me in danger. I ordered my staff to go home, and I shut down the hotel indefinitely. There was no other alternative. It would have to be that way until I ended the feud between Ethan and me for good.

I finished the rest of my workout without interruption, making two hours feel like thirty minutes. After coming out of the women's locker room freshly showered and changed back into usual street attire—leather jacket, jeans, and a ball cap—I spotted the man who had spoken to me earlier. He was also on his way out.

"Hey, you again," he said, flashing that same grin.

"Yes, I'm still the same person."

"Do you work out here often? I ask because I've never seen you here before."

"I take it you're here every day then."

"Pretty much."

"No other obligations?"

"You mean like a job? I work for myself. I trade cryptocurrencies. I know, I know, it sounds like a BS type of job that someone would either say to impress or to blow off the question."

"Exactly, only I didn't really ask what you did for a living."

"No, you didn't. But it was definitely implied. But it's the truth. I'm a trader."

"I see."

"I can tell by the look on your face that I haven't convinced you."

"There's no need to."

"Alright, let's flip this. Tell me what BS job you do for a living."

"I'm a retired assassin."

Quinn let out a laugh. "That's a good one. I like your style. Let's forget about jobs. That's boring talk anyway. How about your name? You never did tell me the last time I asked."

"You're right," I said as I locked eyes with him. It took a beat for him to realize an answer wasn't coming.

"Okay, I get it. Apparently, we're not at that point yet where names are equally shared. That's cool. Maybe we're at the point where we can get something to eat at the same table."

I continued to eye Quinn.

"Come on, you gotta eat, I gotta eat—we'll just do it from across each other."

Realistically, the last thing I needed in my current situation was to have lunch with a man I had just met when countless strangers were trying to kill me. And yet there I was, minutes later, sitting at a table across from him in a small Italian restaurant.

"You're not from New York, are you?" he asked after we placed our orders.

"What makes you say that?"

"My gut. I think you're one of those people that never settle down anywhere for a long time. Always on the move."

"Maybe you're talking about yourself."

"Oh, I'm definitely one of those types. Never in one place for very long."

"Why's that?"

Quinn shrugged. "I've always been that way, I guess. I go wherever the flow takes me."

"And now the flow has brought you to New York." I placed my napkin on my lap.

"It has. I have friends in town."

"How long is your visit?"

"Depends on how long your visit is."

"I hate to disappoint you, but I highly doubt we'll see each other again."

A dramatic frown appeared on Quinn's face. "Say it isn't so?"

"I'm afraid it is. That's life."

"I'm guessing I'll see you at the gym again. You like working out daily. I could see that by your intensity. You'll be back in there soon."

The server brought our meals, and we ate. There was more conversation. Quinn tried to pry information out of me at every corner, but I wasn't giving it to him. He was pleasant and funny. I won't say I didn't enjoy his company, but I had a contract on my head. Anyone around me could end up as collateral damage. And quite frankly, I could count the number of people I trusted on both hands—and Sid Quinn wasn't one of them.

32

After my lunch with Quinn, we parted ways outside the restaurant. I walked in the opposite direction of Willie's building in case Quinn decided to tail me. During that time, I received a call. I didn't recognize the number, but very few people had the number on my current phone, so I answered. I didn't say hello or anything. I simply connected the call and waited quietly. So did the other person—until she cleared her throat.

"Lottie, is that you?" I asked.

"Sei. Thank God it's you. I wasn't sure if this number was still good.

"Is there a problem?"

"No, no, no, not at all. But I do have information I'd like to pass on to you that could be helpful. Remember our contact at the deli? The one who fed us information on Bradford Travers, the one with the yacht?"

"I do."

"Travers is in New York."

"And how do you know that?"

"He visited the deli. Mohamed Abadi, the young man who works there, called me."

"Send me the location of the deli."

"I'm texting the name and address now. Do you remember where Ethan's safe house was located?" she asked.

"I do, but I highly doubt it's still in use. Wasn't it you and Dorothy that compromised it during your last trip to New York?"

"We did, but it might be back in use. I'll send you that address too. Good luck, Sei."

The deli wasn't very far from where I was located, only a fifteen-minute walk. I figured Willie would be okay for a bit longer with Sanka and his crew still there.

New York's Best Deli was located on the corner of Second Avenue and East Third Street. I headed inside and walked up to a man who was sweeping an aisle.

"Excuse me, I'm looking for Mohamed. Is he here today?"

The man paused his sweeping. "I am Mohamed. So is he and he," he said, pointing to two other men.

I remembered Kingsley mentioning that he was a young man. The one speaking looked the most youthful, twenty-five at the most.

"I'm looking for Mohamed Abadi."

"I am him. Have we met before?"

"We have friends in common."

It took a moment, but the look on his face told me he understood what I was talking about.

"May I speak with you in private?" I asked.

"Um, yeah, sure. We can go in the back."

The storeroom was typical for a New York bodega. The shelves were stocked with an abundance of dry goods, and there was a walk-in fridge toward the rear.

"How can I help you?" His eyes avoided mine as he fidgeted with the broom.

"You know Lottie Kingsley, correct?"

"Yes. Is this about the call I made to her earlier?"

"It is. Would you be willing to tell me what happened?"

"Yes. Ms. Kingsley and her friend, I think her name was Dorothy, they wanted information about a man named Kazmer. I didn't know him very well, but I did know the other person. I'm sorry, I don't know his name. I always referred to him as 'my friend.'"

"It's fine. Go on."

"Well, this other man always came into my deli. After Ms. Kingsley came by, I didn't see him again until yesterday. He ordered more food than one person could eat, so he had to be with others."

"Can you confirm who these other people are?"

"I can't, but I do have this."

Mohamed pulled out his phone and then showed me photos of a black motor home.

"He got into this."

"It's a lot of room for one person," I said. "I need a favor, Mohamed. Can you pull the security footage from yesterday?" I asked, looking up at the camera above the door. "And any other cameras you might have inside the store? I'm sure you captured him, and I would like that footage, in addition to those photos on your phone. I am willing to reimburse you for your time."

"Yeah, sure. No problem, I'll get started on it later tonight. Do you want to come back and pick it up on a flash drive, or can I just upload it to a cloud server, and you can download it?"

"Airdrop me those photos right now and upload the security footage to the cloud. I'll give you a number you can text me at when it's ready. Also, you can send me your banking information. When I've received the security footage, I'll transfer a fair payment. I won't negotiate. Do we have a deal?"

"Yes, definitely."

I thought briefly about heading to Ethan's defunct safe house. Still, I'd already been gone from Willie longer than I'd anticipated.

I'll head to Chinatown now. I can come back here later, when it's dark, and look around.

33

On my way back to Willie's place, I studied the photos that Abadi had passed on to me. The motor home had to be a command center for the contract. Travers must have been tracking me across the country. How else would he have ended up in New York at the same time as me? I didn't buy that he was here the entire time, because Abadi said this was the first time he'd seen him in the shop for a while. That told me that he'd just arrived shortly after I did.

Either Travers was right on my tail, or he made a calculated guess based on tracking me that I was heading to New York. There was a chance the assassin sent after me last time, Vegas, mentioned my location.

Travers had probably hired him. And if that was the case, did he know about Willie's place? Had Vegas conveyed that information to him? I picked up the pace. If Travers had knowledge of that information, I'd need a better plan in place.

Willie was napping when I returned, so I looked for Sanka and found him on the roof.

"Sei, everything is moving ahead as planned," he said with a smile. "We are on schedule. I'm just setting up sensors around the perimeter. Once they're activated, you'll be alerted the second anyone sets foot on the roof. I'll have hidden cameras there, there, and there. Not to mention the ones on the building across the road. There are measures we can put in place that can prevent people from accessing the roof, but that will require more time."

"We need to quicken the pace," I said.

"Is there something I should be aware of?" he asked.

"I've just come into information that might have compromised this location."

"I see. How compromised?"

Sanka was unaware of my situation. I'd given Jackson a brief overview of the contract and what I was up against. To my knowledge, I didn't think he'd conveyed any of it to Sanka.

"There's something I need to tell you. It's about why I require all of this additional security."

Sanka held up a hand to stop me. "Sei, I know. Everyone knows about the contract. It's no secret. And don't worry. You can trust my men and me. We are not interested in the bounty. So now that we both understand what is happening, we need to work together."

"Very well, then. I need your honest assessment. The security you're putting in place was more along the lines of bolstering the weak areas of the building, not making this place impenetrable. Is it possible to secure this building from multiple attacks?"

"Sei, I've secured buildings in worse conditions than this one, but this location will never be one hundred percent secure. Someone with the right equipment and know-how will gain entry. But you'll at least know about it before they do. What you really need in place is a solid escape plan, a way for you and Willie to get out undetected."

"Any ideas?"

"Not yet, but I will give it some thought. Are you expecting visitors soon?"

"I can't be sure when, but it's imminent."

"I'll make sure everything we talked about is done today. At the very least, there won't be a welcome mat outside."

I left Sanka to continue with his work. I wanted to have a conversation with Willie. He needed to know the need to abandon his place was a real possibility. I hated that I'd put him in this situation.

Willie had already risen from his nap and was drinking tea on the second floor. I sat next to him and poured myself a cup.

"How was your day, Sei? Did you accomplish what you needed?" he asked.

"I did, but I also received some unpleasant news."

I quickly brought Willie up to speed on Travers.

"Are you one hundred percent sure it's him?" Willie asked.

"I'll know once I receive the security footage from the deli. He was seen entering this motor home."

Willie looked at the photos Abadi had given me.

"He will stand out in New York no matter where he goes."

"You're right about that. I plan to go after him. There is one problem. I can't be sure he doesn't know about this place. He might have hired Vegas to come after me the last time I was here. I don't know if this location was compromised or not."

"Hmmm, I understand what you're saying. I may or may not be the reason why he came to New York the same time as you." Willie took a sip of his tea. "What is it you really want to tell me? Updating me isn't the reason for this conversation."

"We might need to vacate the premises. There is only so much Sanka and his men can do to secure the building. Now that I know Travers is here and is most likely the one updating the live dossier, we run the risk of being exposed."

"I'm not leaving, Sei. This is my home. I trust Sanka's security efforts."

"All I'm saying here is that it might come to it."

"Then do what you can to make sure it doesn't."

34

P egasus drove south along the Bowery. Travers was in the front passenger seat, staring out the window.

"I know we came here because of Chinatown, but really she could be staying anywhere in the city. Any ideas about that?" Gary asked Travers. "I can keep driving around. That's my job, but we ain't blending in, if you haven't noticed. Maybe you and the boys should check into a hotel, and I'll find a place to park Pegasus."

"No go. This is a mobile command unit. We need access at all times. Can't you just park this thing on the street?"

"First, finding street parking is a bitch in New York. Second, New York City law doesn't permit parking an RV on the street for more than twenty-four hours."

"So, move it every twenty-four hours."

"I point you back to my first point about finding parking in the first place. Really, we need a plan. If you're thinking Chinatown, we should just go there."

"Not yet."

"Alright, any luck with people identifying that stairwell that Vegas was killed in?"

"Nothing I think is credible." Travers tapped at his tablet. "I got so many people telling me they know where this stairwell is."

"What makes you think they're wrong?"

"Because I remembered there was one thing Vegas mentioned to me that could be a tip to where he was."

"What's that?"

"He mentioned he was eating almond cookies."

"So?"

"So almond cookies are served in Chinese restaurants or bakeries. That's another clue pointing to Chinatown."

"Let's assume she's in Chinatown right now. That's not far from where we are."

"I know, but like you said earlier, Pegasus doesn't blend. If we start driving up and down those narrow streets, we might as well use a bullhorn and announce that we're looking for Sei. Did you forget what she did back at that casino? It's too dangerous. We need to approach this carefully. Ideally, we need to confirm a location and update the dossier. Let the trained professionals deal with her. Plus, there must be hundreds of stairwells in Chinatown."

"So you're waiting for someone to peg that staircase in Chinatown."

"That's right. If someone gives me a location in Chinatown, we'll send Tran to check it out. He's Asian."

"He's Vietnamese, not Chinese."

Travers rolled his eyes. "He'll blend enough. If it pans out, we'll update the dossier."

He scrolled through messages that people from the message board had sent to him.

"Do you have friends in Chinatown?" Gary asked. "People who can help us out on the ground?"

"No, that's the one place we're dead. Chinatown is a whole

different beast. They protect their own. As outsiders, we won't have much sway."

"Surely, Carmotte has connections."

"I can't go to him for help on this one. I'm already on thin ice with him as it is."

"Money talks. There's got to be someone willing to flip. Maybe send Tran in now. Have him get a feel. It beats driving around and doing nothing."

THIRTY MINUTES LATER, Tran left Pegasus with a pin camera in his sunglasses and a mic taped to his chest. He took long pulls on his vape pen as he walked around Chinatown. His orders from Travers were to get a look at the restaurants and bakeries in the neighborhood. Under no circumstances was he to start asking anyone about Sei or Willie. The first thing that Tran did was slip into a small noodle shop to eat.

"What the hell is he doing?" Travers asked as he stared at the monitor. "Dammit, I knew we should have put an earpiece on him."

"He's probably craving Asian food," Rocha said. "All we eat is Western food. I don't blame him. I could go for some feijoada." Rocha closed his eyes and inhaled. "It's the best. I'll call him on his cell." After a few attempts, he stopped. "He's either got his phone off, or he's ignoring the call."

For the next thirty minutes, they watched a bowl of noodles and an order of spring rolls slowly disappear, all while Travers berated Tran from Pegasus.

"I tell you, bringing this kid on was a mistake."

"He performed well back at the casino," Gary said.

"I don't give a shit. He needs to learn how to listen to every order, not just the ones he feels like."

"He's on the move," Rocha said.

"It's about damn time," Travers said.

From that point on, Tran did reasonably well, stopping at every restaurant to peruse the menus outside and then stepping inside for a moment. When he came across a bakery, he went in and ordered an almond cookie. Something else Travers had requested.

"For someone with a bean pole frame, he can sure eat a lot," Gary mused.

"I hope he brings cookies back for us," Rocha said. "They look good."

"I second that," Gary said. "Watching him eat is making me hungry."

"Enough with the food talk, all right?" Travers snapped.

Tran exited a bakery munching on an almond cookie and then made a call on his cell phone. Rocha's phone rang.

"Oh, now he decides to check in," Travers said.

He snatched the phone from Rocha, putting it on speakerphone.

"Just what the hell do you think you're doing?"

"I do what you ask. I looking at restaurants and bakeries," Tran said, his high voice jumping up an octave. "You want me to do something else?"

"No, stop sidetracking."

"What do you mean 'sidetracking?'"

"Never mind. Keep looking." Travers disconnected the call.

"You want me to go walk with him?" Rocha asked. "I could pass as a tourist."

"No, I want you to stay here."

Tran stood outside of the bakery while he finished his cookie. Across the street, the pin camera picked up a motorcycle parked on the sidewalk. Travers leaned in for a closer look.

"Son of a bitch. I don't believe it. Does that motorcycle look like the bike Sei rode away on from the casino?"

"Maybe," Gary said.

"Pull up the security cam footage we have of her leaving the casino."

Rocha tapped at his keyboard, and a few seconds later, the footage was playing on the monitor.

"Pause it! It's looking pretty similar to me."

By then, Tran had already walked away from the location. "Get that kid back on the phone."

Rocha dialed, and Tran answered.

"Tran, go back to the bakery you were at!" Travers shouted. "Across the street, there's a black motorcycle. Go get a good look at it."

Tran did as he was told. He headed back, crossed over to the other side, and approached the bike. He looked it over carefully, giving the three men a good look at that motorcycle.

"No license plates," Travers said. "What about the footage? Does that motorcycle have plates?"

Rocha scrolled through the footage until they got a look at the rear of the bike driving off. It didn't have plates.

"Holy shit!" Travers exclaimed. "I can't fricking believe it. That's her bike. Duc, step back to the other side of the street and give us a look at the buildings across the way."

Tran did that and gave sweeping views both horizontally and vertically.

"What's his location?" Travers asked.

"He's on Doyers street. You want me to update the dossier?"

"No, not yet. Let's keep an eye on the place for a little bit and see if we can get confirmation. Duc? You still there?"

"Yes, boss."

"Go back to that bakery across the street and camp out there. Don't leave under any circumstances."

35

Tran sat in the bakery while keeping an eye on the buildings across the street. In the meantime, Rocha gathered information on the businesses and residents living on Doyers. Gary drove Pegasus in a wide loop around Chinatown, switching up the streets every now and then to not create too much of a pattern.

"Anything newsworthy?" Travers asked as he came up behind Rocha.

"I'm working on gathering as much info as I can on the ground-level businesses. That doesn't mean there aren't smaller ones on the higher floors. I want to be thorough. Once I'm sure I've got the businesses covered, I'll work on the upper floors and the residents and find out who owns the buildings. Most businesses are normal for the neighborhood: restaurants, Chinese medicine shops, laundry, internet cafés, printers, clothing and electronic shops. I don't see anything out of the ordinary. The owners I've identified so far don't have any connection to our world, and none of the businesses have been in the news for any sort of illicit activities."

"Who owns that internet café right across the street? Her bike is parked near the entrance."

"I don't know yet."

"Well, shift your efforts to finding out everything you can about Excellent Cyber & Print Café."

When five o'clock rolled around, Tran rang Rocha telling him the bakery was closing, and asked what he should do.

"Do you want him to wait outside on the sidewalk?" Rocha asked as he eyed Travers for an answer.

"No, it might draw attention. Tell him to meet us at the corner of Doyers and Bowery. We'll pick him up."

A short time later, Tran hopped back on board Pegasus with a large bag of almond cookies.

"I buy all the cookies they had. It's so good." Tran passed the bag around.

"What do we know about Excellent Cyber & Print Café?" Travers asked through a mouthful.

"In the last three years, that shop changed their name twelve times. I don't know who the owner is yet. But the building also changed hands twelve times during that same three years."

"Who owns the building now?"

"W. W. Woo Woo."

"What?" Crinkles appeared on Travers's forehead.

"That's what it says. Two W initials, and I'm guessing Woo Woo is the surname. I don't know."

"I need information that helps. Not the stuff you're turning over," Travers barked back.

"Why don't we just go inside?" Tran asked. "What the problem? I go make some copies or use internet café. I can stay there and game for a few hours and keep watch on the place."

"That's a good idea," Rocha said. "Tran can blend."

Travers took a minute to think through the situation. Half of him believed Sei was holed up somewhere on that block. Half of him didn't want to do anything that would make Carmotte look bad. Updating the dossier with a Chinatown location would trigger a bunch of assassins and gangsters from New York. If it was going down and law enforcement got involved, he wanted Sei dead.

Travers walked to the front of the motor home. "What do you think, Gary? Can you foresee anything backfiring from this?"

Gary had been with Travers for a while. He'd seen Travers at his highs and his lows. And he always had a pragmatic way of looking at the situation with a sense of neutrality.

"I know you want to update the dossier, but if it's the wrong place and a bunch of innocent people get caught in this mess, that's not going to look good, and it'll bring a ton of heat down on Chinatown. It won't hurt to send Tran in for an hour or so. If it starts getting weird, we pull him out."

Travers glanced at his watch; it was coming up on 6:30 p.m. At the moment, sending Tran in was the best option they had. But it was also risky—if Sei was in there, she'd be on high alert. Tran's mission could end up being one way. *That's a risk I'm comfortable taking.*

"Okay, Duc. You got the green light. Go game for an hour. But this time, keep your phone on in case we need to contact you. You'll wear the same glasses and mic, plus an earpiece. And don't get too involved in the game. You're there to conduct surveillance. Got it?"

"Yes, boss."

36

It was half-past five when Willie invited me to have an early dinner with him at Dee Dee's.

"I have a shortcut to the restaurant, Sei," he said.

Willie led me to a small door that I had always assumed housed a closet or storage space. Behind the door was a spiral staircase.

"Does the building have other secrets I should know of?" I asked.

The stairwell led down to another door. Willie opened it, revealing the restaurant's kitchen. I made a mental note to let Sanka know that one more entrance needed to be secured. It also occurred to me this might be a perfect back door out of the building, should it come to that.

We stepped into a kitchen full of cooks hurriedly preparing the numerous varieties of dim sum sold in the restaurant. This particular restaurant had sixty different types of delectable snack dishes on offer—no small feat keeping up with that demand. As we made our way through the kitchen, not a single person paid us any attention. We passed through a pair of swinging doors into the main dining room. It was a busy night at Dee Dee's. From what I could see, every table was occupied.

A young man approached and bowed slightly. "I have a table waiting," he said.

Willie and I were led to a small corner table that had been out of my initial line of sight. It was toward the rear of the dining area, away from the other tables.

"Is this your private table?" I asked Willie.

He nodded.

I wasn't surprised by his answer, since he owned the building.

"Who's the owner?"

Just then, an elderly woman wearing a red blouse with white pants approached us. She had short, permed hair, wore gold-framed glasses, and had a cheery smile on her face.

"Willie, so good to see you here tonight. Who's your friend?"

"Dee Dee, please meet my niece, Michelle."

Willie never introduced me by my real name.

"Michelle, welcome to Dee Dee's. Is this your first time here?"

"First time dining here, but I have tried the food previously. It's always been delicious."

"I'm pleased to hear that. Enjoy your dinner."

After Dee Dee left, I asked Willie if she was really the owner.

Willie smiled. "We're partners. Is that an okay answer for you?"

"I'll be right back. I'm fine with whatever you order."

I walked back into the kitchen and quickly found what I was looking for—a door leading out the back.

Behind the building was a narrow walkway, big enough for people to squeeze through. The wet ground was littered with debris I didn't care to identify. The air had a sour stench, possibly due to piles of overstuffed plastic trash bags. Steam rose from a manhole not far from me. I looked up and saw a metal fire escape clinging to Willie's building. I didn't notice this from inside, and now I understood why. At no point along the fire escape was there an entry point to the building. *Willie must have had the windows bricked up.*

I explored the length of the walkway. To the north, it opened up onto Pell Street, which intersected with Doyers, where Willie's shop and restaurant were located. Heading south, the walkway funneled out onto the Bowery, a busy thoroughfare that ran north and south through Manhattan.

When I returned, there was a pot of tea already on the table along with bamboo containers containing dumplings, rolled rice noodles, stuffed tofu skins, garlic steamed spareribs, spring rolls, black bean meatballs, and more.

I hadn't realized how hungry I was until the smell of the dishes hit my nose. I picked up my chopsticks and helped myself to a soup dumpling, one of Mui's favorites. It's essentially seasoned pork and hot soup tucked inside a paper-thin wrapper.

"Do you have plans tonight?" Willie asked.

"I want to search for the motor home. It won't be easy to hide it, and I would rather surprise Travers than have him surprise us. Was there something you needed me to do?"

"I was simply inquiring. It's nice having you around."

"Thank you, Willie. But my presence isn't a good thing. I hope to be out of your way sooner rather than later."

"Yes, let us both wish this business with Ethan is put behind us."

I ate quickly and excused myself from Willie. He knew many of the customers dining at the restaurant and had plenty of company. I got back up to my bedroom via the secret staircase and retrieved my backpack and bike helmet. I bumped into Sanka on the way out.

"Sanka, there's another entrance that I didn't know about. Come with me."

I led him to the staircase, walked him up and down, and showed him the back exit into the walkway.

"I think this will make a perfect escape route."

He nodded. "I can secure the door so that it's one way. You and Willie will be able to exit, but no one will be able to come back in. I'll put sensors on the door in case someone tries to breach it."

"What about the kitchen staff bumping into it?"

"That won't be enough. Someone would have to be breaking through the door to trigger the sensors. I've already installed a cameras in the walkway behind the building. So you're already covered there."

I thanked Sanka and left. My plan was to head over to Ethan's safe house to see whether it was back in working order or not. There was also hope that the black motorhome might be parked nearby.

A short time later, I arrived at the street where the safe house was located. It was four blocks away from the deli where Abadi worked. It just so happened I received a text message from Abadi at that time. He was ready to upload the security footage from the deli. I sent him a link to a secure cloud storage folder and waited. When I accessed the deli footage, I was able to confirm the man Abadi referenced was indeed Travers.

37

Tran made his way up the narrow staircase that led to the Excellent Cyber & Print Café. There was no one behind the counter, so he tapped the silver bell a couple of times and waited. A few minutes later, a man with brown skin and dread-locks appeared in the doorway from behind a cloth curtain, holding a toolbox.

"What are you doing here?" he asked with an accent that Tran couldn't place.

"I want to use the internet." Tran pointed at the small neon sign that read Cyber Café

"Um, I think we're closed."

"Why close? Downstairs sign says open."

"Wait." The man poked his head through the curtained doorway and called out. "Sanka, come here."

A minute passed before another man with a similar look appeared.

"What is it?" Sanka asked.

"This kid wants to use the internet."

A frown appeared on Sanka's face. "How did he get inside?"

"I was still working on the front door. I came up to get more tools."

Sanka turned to Tran. "Sorry, you have to come back another time."

"But I want to play game. Let me use internet."

"Sorry. We're closed."

Tran continued to argue that the sign downstairs said the shop was open. Finally, Sanka relented and said Tran could use the computer for an hour. He led Tran to the small room where five computers were set up. Tran plopped down into a chair and started playing games. Outside the room, Sanka told the man to keep an eye on the gamer and then kick him out at exactly one hour.

FROM INSIDE PEGASUS, Travers wasn't pleased with what he was seeing. Even though Tran had persuaded the men to let him in, the room he was in was shut off from everything else. And it was dark, just dim lighting around the edges of the room.

Travers and Gary were both standing over Rocha and staring at the live feed from Tran's glasses.

"Does the name Sanka ring a bell to you?" Gary asked.

"I never heard it. Gil, see if you can dig up anything on a Sanka."

"He needs to get out of that room. We can't see anything."

"Duc, can you hear me?" Travers asked as he spoke into the mic that fed the earpiece Tran wore.

"Yeah, boss. What do you want?"

"I need you to walk around. We can't see shit in that room."

"But I'm playing a game."

"Duc, if you don't get your ass off that seat and look around, I'll make sure that keyboard is the last one you ever touch."

"Okay, okay. Relax."

Tran got up and left the room.

"And stop looking around jerky," Travers said. "It's hard for us to see. Slow, sweeping movements."

Tran left the room and ran right into the man who had first greeted him.

"What are you doing? Why aren't you playing your game?" he asked.

"I need to pee. Where is bathroom?"

The man scratched the back of his head. "You can't hold it?"

"What the problem? I am customer. I can't use bathroom?"

"Alright, but you need to be fast. Come on."

The man led Tran into a larger room filled with antique Chinese furniture. In the center was a round table surrounded with chairs.

"Slow down." Tran heard Travers whisper into the mic. "And look around so we can see everything."

Tran did just that and fell behind.

"Hey, keep up," the man said, looking over his shoulder. "You need to be quick."

"It's just some stupid dining room," Travers said.

"He will probably need to get himself on the other floors," Gary said.

"Duc, you need to figure out how to get on the upper floors."

The man pointed to a small bathroom, and Tran went inside and groomed himself in the mirror before calling out to the man. "Hey, you still there?"

"Yeah, what is it?"

"No toilet paper in here."

"You told me you had to pee."

"Yeah, but now I take a shit. I need toilet paper. You want me to get shit all over your chair when I go back to my computer?"

Everyone inside Pegasus heard the man groan on the other side of the door before hearing footsteps walk away.

"Now! Go look around!" Travers shouted.

Tran slipped out of the bathroom.

"Where you want me go?" Tran whispered into his mic.

"Find a stair," Travers answered. "There! Straight ahead."

Tran took the stairs to the next floor two at a time. When he reached the top, he heard men talking with the same accent as the other two. He peeked out from the stairwell and saw a large open room with sitting chairs, a sofa, and a coffee table. There was a closed door at the far end of the room. Standing near a couple of large windows was the man Tran had met earlier, Sanka. He was speaking with another man.

"Boss, what you want me do?" Tran whispered into the mic.

"It looks like those men are securing that window," Rocha said, "You can see the sensors they're installing."

"Duc, get out of there," Travers said. "Come back to Pegasus."

"Okay, boss." The visual on the screen went black as Tran had removed his glasses.

"Only one reason to secure the place," Gary said. "Sei has to be there."

"That's right," Travers said. "Gil, update the dossier. Let us watch hell rain down on her."

38

L ocating Ethan's safe house was easy, thanks to the location and description Kingsley had sent me. There wasn't a black motor home parked outside or anywhere on the block. And from the look of the dark building, it still appeared to be abandoned. There was a lockbox on the front door, but the glass window off to the side had been broken. I climbed inside.

Once inside, I made my way up to the second floor. None of the light switches worked, but enough ambient light shone through the windows for me to see well enough, and my eyes had already adjusted to the dark.

There were seven closed doors on the floor. Four of them were unlocked, and the other three were locked. Each floor had the same number of rooms with an array of locked and unlocked doors. When I reached the top floor, I still hadn't found anything of interest.

There's nothing here, Sei.

I was on my way back down, between the third and second floors, when I heard an unusual noise. I froze. It sounded like footsteps in the stairwell. And it stopped right about the same time I did. Under my leather jacket, I wore the utility belt that held my throwing knives. I removed one before peeking over the railing. I didn't see anything, but that didn't mean I was alone.

My gut continued to sound the alarm. I stepped back into the hallway and into a nearby room that had an open door. With my back up against the wall near the entrance, I waited.

A creak echoed in the hall. Someone was definitely in the building with me. It didn't matter whether it was a professional or a scavie. Either one would fail. But the heavy footsteps I heard approaching told me it wasn't a professional. My estimate: This person was five steps away, and there was only one of them.

Many before you have tried. All have failed.

Four steps.

I hope you said your goodbyes.

Three steps.

Enjoy your last breath.

Two steps.

The person stopped just outside the room. I tightened my grip around the knife handle.

Let's get it over with, Sei.

As I was about to step into the hall and punch the blade through that unfortunate person's neck, my nose caught a familiar scent: cologne.

I shot out of the room with my left arm straight out, slamming my palm into a man's chest and pushing him back into the wall behind him, hard. He groaned. A second later, I had the knife pressed against his throat.

"What are you doing here?" I growled.

"Hey, take it easy. Let me go."

The mystery man was Quinn, the man I'd met earlier at the gym.

"If I press any harder, this blade will cut into your throat. I'd answer my question if I were you."

"Okay, okay. You caught me. I was following you."

"Why?"

"I don't know. By chance, I saw you on your motorcycle riding down the street."

"I had a helmet on. How did you know it was me?"

"I have the image of your body burned into my memory. I mean, I didn't really know, but I was like eighty percent sure it was you. So I followed you on my mountain bike."

"And?"

"I followed you until you stopped at the corner of the street outside. When you removed your helmet, I saw it was you."

"And?"

"My plan was to catch up and surprise you, but then I saw you go into this spooky ass building."

"You make a habit of following people into strange buildings?"

"Cute ones," he laughed hesitantly.

I removed the blade from Quinn's throat. He wasn't on the contract. He was too naïve to be.

The expression on his face twisted as he reached around and rubbed his back. "You're stronger than you look."

"I'm a lot of things."

"Where did you learn how to handle a knife like that?"

"I took a night class."

"Ha. Ha. Funny. Okay, next question. Why did you come into this empty building? Are you the owner?"

"You ask a lot of questions."

"That's me trying to spark a conversation."

"Stop trying."

I walked around Quinn and headed to the stairs.

"Wait! Where are you off to?"

"Home. And you should too."

"But, the night's young. You're by yourself, and I'm by myself.

Makes complete sense for us to stick together and keep each other company, don't you think?"

I stopped and turned to face Quinn.

"You were seconds away from bleeding out in this hallway. You do realize that, right?"

He shrugged. "Honestly, I didn't think you'd actually go through with it."

I crinkled my brow. "What makes you so sure of that?"

"I can tell you like me."

I rolled my eyes before heading downstairs. "Go home, Quinn."

"How about dinner? You need to eat."

"I've had dinner," I said as I walked toward the entrance of the building.

"Okay, what about a drink? I know this nice rooftop bar that has great views of the city. It's totally casual. You're fine the way you are."

I stopped in my tracks. "What's wrong with the way I'm dressed?"

"Nothing. I'm just saying. Some places in the city have a strict dress code. This isn't one of those places. You and I are both fine."

"I'm not interested." I pulled the front door open and exited the building. "Don't follow me, Quinn. I might not be so forgiving the next time."

I hurried back to my motorcycle and put my helmet back on. I didn't see Quinn anywhere, nor did I see the mountain bike he claimed to have been riding. Letting him go was the right thing to do. He had no idea what he was getting himself involved with. In hindsight, I should have never accepted his invitation to lunch.

I hope you stay away, Quinn...for your safety.

39

Travers no longer cared if Pegasus stood out like a sore thumb. Nor did he care if Sei figured out he was inside. He knew she would eventually work out who he was. She'd laid eyes on him when he was involved with her daughter's abduction—no forgetting that. However, what Travers wanted most of all was to redeem himself in Carmotte's eyes. What better way to do that than by documenting Sei's demise.

"Park Pegasus on Doyers Street," Travers told Gary.

"Are you sure?"

"Very much so. Gil, make sure you got the cameras aimed at the building and the entrance. I don't want to miss anything. I want it all captured."

"What if she comes out after us?" Gil asked.

"Pegasus is a fortress. She can't get inside. Gary, just make sure we can get out of here in a jiffy if NYPD makes an appearance."

"Might I suggest a better location? Those streets are too narrow for Pegasus to maneuver through quickly if all hell breaks loose. The farther away, the better."

"I need to see what's happening." Travers grabbed Gil's shirt collar and yanked him to his feet. "I have a job for you. How fast can you set up a few cameras covering the building?"

"Fifteen minutes, maybe."

"Do that now. Hurry!"

Gil exited Pegasus in a jiffy with the necessary equipment.

"Perfect," Gary said. "When he comes back, I'll find us a safe spot to camp out."

Travers leaned down and spoke into a mic. "Duc, where the hell are you? I thought I told you to get out of there."

Tran didn't answer.

"Why isn't he answering? If that kid went back to the toilet to finish his shit, I'm going to lose it. Duc, answer me. Where are you?" Travers shouted into the mic. "Is the mic even on?"

"Hard to tell, but if we can't hear anything from him," Gary said with a shrug, "probably compromised. He probably got pinched by one of those men on his way out."

"You think?" Travers said as he shook his head in disappointment.

"What do you want to do?" Gary asked.

"We're not doing anything. If Duc couldn't get out on his own, that's on him."

"We should at least make an effort. We might need him later."

Travers let out an exaggerated breath. "Oh, all right. The things you make me do. Go get him."

"Why me?" Gary asked.

"You said you wanted to help Duc, so figure out how it's going to be done."

"I'm not going inside, and that's final," Gary said. "I got a better idea. When Gil comes back, we'll have him update the dossier. We'll tell people they'll get a bonus if they secure Duc. Not much, maybe ten grand."

Travers mulled over the suggestion. "Okay, but it should be five. I've got a budget to stick to."

It didn't take long before Rocha had the cameras up and running and was back inside Pegasus, breathing hard. Per Travers's orders, he quickly updated the dossier with Tran's photo.

"Did you ever locate a photo of Willie?" Travers asked.

"Yeah," Rocha answered.

"Good. Upload that as well. Add him to the list of people to die and make it a five-thousand-dollar bonus."

"You're sure? He's just an old man," Gil said. "Check it out."

He put Willie's photo on the monitor.

"Is this recent?" Travers asked as he looked at the frail, elderly man.

"It's got to be, because he looks pretty old to me."

Gary nudged Travers and pointed to another monitor broadcasting a live shot of the front of the building. "Check it out."

A group of people had gathered outside of the dim sum restaurant. They appeared to be saying their farewells to each other. One of the individuals was an old man hunched over with a cane.

"Hey, that looks like Willie," Gil said as he looked back and forth between the live feed and the photo.

"That's definitely him," Gary added.

"I just had a thought," Travers said.

"And what's that?" Gary asked.

"I need you two to do something. Don't worry, it won't kill you."

40

S anka stepped on the pair of glasses and twisted his boot, snapping the frame and shattering the glass. Before that, he'd destroyed a mini microphone camera and earpiece. Tran sat on the floor with his back against the wall. He was using his shirt collar to stem the flow of blood from his nostrils. A group of tall men, each twice his body weight, stood around him.

"Stand him up," Sanka said calmly.

One of Sanka's men grabbed Tran's arms and jerked him back to his feet. Tran kept his head turned down, avoiding Sanka's eyes.

Sanka wound up and delivered another backhand to Tran's face, lifting him off his feet and into the wall behind him. He fell to the floor, dazed. The same man lifted Tran back to his feet. Another man grabbed Tran's head and forced him to look up at Sanka.

"I will ask one more time. Who are you, and why are you here?"

"I tell you already. My name is Duc Tran."

"I am not interested in your name."

Sanka punched Tran's stomach hard, causing Tran to double over and fall back down to the floor as he gasped for air.

"If you continue to give me stupid answers. I will continue to hurt you until you're dead. Who are you?"

"My boss is Mr. Travers."

"First name."

"Bradford Travers."

"And what do you do for him?"

"I'm a hacker. I do whatever he wants."

"And he sent you here?"

Tran nodded.

"What kind of information did he want you to obtain?"

"He wanted to know if Sei was here."

Sanka looked at his men. "Do a check. Quickly!"

The men disappeared, leaving Sanka alone with Tran. Sanka used his boot to roll Tran to his side so he could look him in his face.

"What is your boss's plan? And don't bullshit me, or I will crush your face."

"If Sei is here, he will tell the others—the people he hired to kill her. That's all I know. I promise."

As I RODE up and down the streets looking for the motor home, the obvious had dawned on me: Travers was a target, but the real threat was the dossier. If Travers even had the slightest hunch of where I might be, all he needed to do was update the dossier. There were plenty of professionals in New York and even more scavies willing to try their luck.

As confident as I felt about defending myself, an army of men was still an army of men. Keeping Willie safe in a situation like that would be difficult. And there was only so much Sanka and his men could do to secure the building. I had focused too much on eliminating Ethan's inner circle and developed tunnel vision—again.

Willie needs to be relocated to a hotel outside of Manhattan. And if I need to force him, I will.

I headed back to Willie's place quickly. I wanted him out of there that night. Before heading up to the apartment, I went looking for Willie in the restaurant. His table was empty and had been cleared of dishes.

"Willie left a while ago." The man who seated us earlier had appeared. "Last I saw him, he was outside saying goodbye to a few friends."

"Thank you."

I headed into the kitchen to use the secret staircase, but the door was locked. Sanka had already dealt with it. I walked out of the restaurant and tried the front entrance, but it had already been switched out with a new door, which was locked. I sent Sanka a text and he came down to let me in.

"I'm glad you're back. We have a problem."

GARY RELOCATED Pegasus to a quiet location outside of Chinatown. With the surveillance cameras Gil had set up, they had unobstructed views of the building and all of Doyers. In addition, Travers had the drones that Gil could fly around to provide additional coverage. And best of all, he had leverage.

Gary had no problem escorting Willie back to Pegasus. It wasn't like Willie had the strength or the willingness to fight back. Willie sat quietly in a chair toward the rear of Pegasus. He wasn't tied up or gagged—no need for that as of yet. Travers took a seat next to him.

"Do you have any idea who I am?"

"You're the one called Travers."

Travers's eyebrows shot up. "That's correct. I see Sei shared some information with you."

"What do you want from me?" Willie asked.

"It's my understanding that you are a master at procuring information. Am I right?"

Willie remained silent.

"Your silence speaks volumes. Tell me, what do you know? I want to hear just how good you are at your job."

"Then I will disappoint you, because I haven't learned much yet."

"Oh, come now. Let's not start off by lying to one another just yet. It's so early. I'll make it easy with a few pointed questions. The Black men inside your building, are they your security team? Are they there to shore up the building's defenses?" Travers balled his fists and playfully jabbed for added effect. "Come on, no need to hold on to your secrets."

"You are asking questions you already know the answer to."

"When you put it that way, you're absolutely right. And now you've given me confirmation. Oh, how I do love to be right. Next question: Does Sei know about Pegasus?" Travers motioned to the motor home.

"She knows you're tracking her. She's not stupid."

"Ah, then that means she probably knows I'm also in New York. I take it she's not in the building. I bet she's out looking for me. What about the dossier? I'll assume you were both aware of it and have been checking for updates. Have you checked it lately? Like, say in the last hour or so? No? Ah, okay then, you're not aware of the most recent update, the one that lets everyone know the current location of Sei. If you think about it, me taking you like I did was actually a favor. Do you know how many assassins are on their way to Chinatown as we speak? Someone like you could easily become collateral damage because, I'll tell you, it will be a bloodbath—a show worth watching. And you know what the best part of it is?" Travers motioned toward the monitors. "It's happening live right there. You and I, why, we have front row seats."

S anka led Sei to the second-floor bathroom, which now had a bar across the door with a padlock securing it.

"I locked him up in the bathroom because I didn't know what else to do," he said as he unlocked the door and opened it.

The skinny Asian kid sat on the floor sandwiched between the wall and the toilet. He had bruising and slight swelling across his face. I shut the door to the bathroom and Sanka locked it again.

"The Vietnamese kid's name is Duc Tran, or so he says," Sanka said. "He confirmed that his boss is that Travers guy you mentioned. He even said they were parked nearby. I checked, but I didn't see the motor home he spoke about. Did you?"

"I didn't."

"I hate to break it to you, Sei, but he knows where you are. He probably wanted confirmation. Unfortunately, me keeping this kid here and cutting off his communication gave him his answer."

"How much more work do you and your men need to do?"

"I'd say we're about eighty-five percent done."

"Where are the weak spots?"

"The wiring on the roof isn't complete, but the new door is in place. But it won't withstand a blast. You're also vulnerable from the kitchen. We put a deadbolt on that door, but if someone wants to get through, they will."

"And the windows?"

"The fourth and third floor have bulletproof glass in place. But as a general rule, stay away from the windows. Even the bulletproofed ones won't stop an anti-armor sniper rifle. We weren't able to finish the window on the second floor. I recommend you keep the blinds shut on those." Sanka fidgeted nervously.

"What is it?"

"Look, Sei, I'll help you out as much as I can, but I can't ask my guys to get involved in your beef. I need to cut them loose."

"I understand. Is Willie upstairs in his bedroom?"

"I haven't seen him since you two left for dinner."

I nodded and then made my way to Willie's bedroom on the fourth floor. The lights were off, but I didn't see a shape on the bed.

"Willie?" I called out.

I felt the bed. It was cool to the touch. In the bathroom, the shower and sink were dry. Willie hadn't been there since getting ready for dinner. I pulled out my cell phone and navigated to the website hosting the dossier. It had been updated and named Willie's building as my current location. There was also a bonus for recovering Tran.

I returned to the bathroom. Tran was sitting on the floor and resting his arms and head on top of the seat cover.

"Where's Willie?" I asked, nudging him with my shoe.

"How would I know? I've been in here."

"But you know Willie?"

"I don't know him. I just hear my boss say his name."

I pulled out my phone and used the app Sanka had given me

to watch a recorded video of the outside of the building. I hopped around from the different camera positions until I landed on one that gave me a view of the outside of the restaurant and Doyers Street. I fast-forwarded through the footage until I saw a man set up surveillance cameras across the street. A little later, I watched Willie exit the restaurant. A Caucasian man who wasn't Travers grabbed Willie and forced him away.

"You do know no one is coming for you, right? Travers has left you for dead. They're not planning on rescuing you. Your real role was to be a distraction. They wanted Willie. I bet you didn't realize that."

"That's not true. I came here to confirm you were here."

I showed Tran the footage of Willie being taken.

"Do you really think Travers is that stupid? He didn't need confirmation."

"You don't know that."

"I know more than you think. You're nothing but a pawn in his game."

Tran didn't answer me.

"You realize that, at any minute, very dangerous people will be descending on this place. Have you heard of the term collateral damage? That's what you'll become."

Just then, Sanka and his men appeared. I closed the bathroom door.

"I need one last favor. Travers's men set up cameras across the street. I need them dismantled."

"No problem. I'll destroy them on the way out. What will you do?"

"Travers has Willie. His abduction was picked up by one of the cameras you installed. I have to find that motor home."

"Can you use the kid as leverage?"

"He's worthless to me in that way. I'm just trying to figure out if he knows where Travers might be right now or where he is heading. He can't be that far."

"Is there anything else we can do?"

"You've done more than enough. Leave before you can't."

I followed Sanka and his men down the stairs to the front door.

"Take care, Sei," he said before walking out.

I secured the door and headed back to the bathroom where Tran was.

"Have you given any thought to what I said earlier?" I asked as I stood in the doorway.

"I'm already dead. Why should I help you?"

"You're not dead just yet. There is the possibility that you will make it out of this mess alive, but only if you help me track down that motor home. Do that for me, and I'll make sure you don't die in this bathroom."

Tran didn't answer.

"I'm assuming you've seen the footage from the casino. Am I correct?"

Tran nodded.

"Then you already know I'm more than capable of holding up my end of our agreement. I think you're smart enough to know you don't want to be on the wrong side of me. I'll only ask once more. Do we have a deal?"

Tran nodded. "Deal."

42

I made it very clear to Tran that he would die a most painful death if he double-crossed me. If he tried to run from me, he'd die a painful death. If he did anything that strayed from our agreement, he'd die a painful death. He seemed to have gotten the point, because he listened to everything I said from the moment I let him out of the bathroom.

My plan was to turn Tran loose in the computer room. He said he would try to hack into Pegasus.

While Tran got to work, I headed into my bedroom to gear up. I loaded my utility belt with everything it could hold: an extra magazine, throwing knives, a garrote, a mini-flashlight, and a pair of night-vision glasses. I strapped on two hip holsters, screwed the suppressors to my handguns, and then tucked them in. I slung the strap attached to the sniper rifle over my body. Lastly, I grabbed the mini assault rifle.

Just then, my cell phone buzzed. A sensor on the roof had been tripped. I navigated to the cameras on the top and spotted three men crouched near an AC unit. They looked like scavies. I made my way up the steps leading to the door that opened onto the rooftop.

The three individuals were still crouched near the AC unit. It looked like they were in discussion of their next steps. They were definitely scavies and most likely members of one of the gangs in New York City.

THE PETITE WOMAN had ponytails and wore a light blue, knee-length dress with puffy sleeves and a white pinafore—reminiscent of Alice in *Alice in Wonderland* but with a bit of sexy schoolgirl mixed in. She had just climbed out of a car that was blasting K-pop and filled with people dressed in similar cosplay fashion.

"Farewell," she sang out in her childlike voice as she waved to her friends.

Once the car had disappeared from view, the young woman slipped into the shadows of a nearby building and pulled up her dress to reveal a drop leg holster around her thigh. Tucked inside the holster was a Ruger SR40c compact handgun. Strapped around her other thigh was a knife holster carrying three throwing knives. The woman removed the handgun and released the magazine to examine it before locking it back in place. She holstered the gun and crept down Doyers Street.

Jeong-Ja was an assassin from South Korea who had arrived in the States a week earlier for one specific purpose: to capture the bounty on Sei's head. Secondly, she wanted to attend Comic Con in New York—hence the cosplay outfit, which really wasn't that far off from her everyday fashion.

Jeong-Ja dipped into a dark entranceway in a building and checked her phone. She had already loaded the address of the location into a map app. The blue beacon indicated the building where Sei was purported to be was thirty yards away. There was no foot traffic on the street. A few of the small apartments that lined the upper floors of the buildings had light emanating from their windows.

Sei has to know her location was compromised. She can't be that stupid.

Jeong-Ja knew of Sei, but had never met her in person. She was a little girl when she'd first heard of the deadly woman with cat-like stealth. From that day forward, Jeong-Ja wanted nothing more than to be like Sei. She still did, even at twenty years old. The chance to finally be in Sei's presence produced a flutter of butterflies in her stomach. It was unfortunate that the situation was what it was.

Rather than approach the building from the front, Jeong-Ja looped back around and found a pathway behind the buildings. The uneven asphalt was marked with puddles of water and an array of debris. Giant rats scurried back and forth from the numerous trash piles, unperturbed by her presence.

A few minutes later, Jeong-Ja reached the building where Sei was said to be. Clinging to the building was an old metal fire escape. She climbed up onto a stack of crates and leaped up, gripping the bottom rail of a ladder. She pulled herself up and carefully made her way up the rickety escape.

Every so often, it would clang against the brick building, and Jeong-Ja would freeze. Surprisingly, where there should be windows, there were none. They'd been filled in with bricks. She continued her climb to the roof.

I CAREFULLY UNLOCKED the door leading out to the rooftop while still watching the three individuals through the app. Sanka's technology had made my job so much easier. None of the skills I'd developed over the years were required. I quickly slipped outside and tucked myself into the shadows of the bulkhead that housed the stairs. The three sitting ducks weren't very far from me, but a couple of rooftop water tanks blocked my view, so I continued to monitor them with the app.

What are you waiting for? You've been crouched there longer than need be.

One of the men turned toward the camera. He had a cell phone pressed against his ear.

Are you waiting for instructions?

After a few more seconds of watching, I understood why they weren't moving. They weren't waiting for instructions; they were giving them. The man on the phone pointed at the building across the street and then over to the bulkhead. My eyes scanned the rooftops on the other side of Doyers Street. I would bet my life a sniper was setting up across the way.

I slowly slipped the sniper rifle slung across my back over my head and used the night vision sights to search the tops of the buildings. All but one of the buildings was four stories tall. The other building had five stories. A sniper could be on the roof or in any one of the windows of the fifth floor. I slowly panned across the six dark windows. The windows were all shut, but that didn't mean anything. And most likely, he was lying flat further back in the room. At least, that's how I would have done it. The sights on the rifle were equipped with night vision only, so they wouldn't pick up on a heat signature, which was what I needed if he was far back in a room. Even the night vision goggles I had were useless in that scenario.

After searching the remaining rooftops, I was 99.9% sure a sniper had nested in one of those top apartments. Unless I could draw him out without revealing my location, it would be a long night of wait and see. I needed a distraction.

JEONG-JA REACHED the last level of the fire escape. Because of her tiny stature, the parapet's ledge that ran along the rooftop was out of reach. To reach the roof, she'd need to climb on top of the narrow railing of the fire escape and leap up. Whether or not her grip would be strong enough to pull her up was an entirely different question. The drop to the pavement below was a one-way ticket.

She ran a hand across the railing. There was slight condensation, and she used her dress to wipe the railing dry before climbing on top of it. She tested the grip of her white trainers—no slippage. She always wore trainers, even with her cosplay outfits. She made a mistake once of wearing heels. She nearly paid with her life when a mark for a contract almost got the best of her when she lost her footing.

Jeong-Ja crouched and leaped with her arms stretched upwards. Her hands gripped the edge of the brick parapet perfectly, and she pulled herself up so she could see over the ledge. Directly in front of her was a tall wooden water tower that blocked the moonlight above. She pulled herself up and over the parapet and onto the rooftop.

She peered through the legs that supported the water tank, searching for the bulkhead that housed the stairs. It was right about then that she spotted movement. Kneeling next to a large AC unit was a man. Jeong-Ja smiled. *Competition?*

He had his back to her. Rookie move number one.

He was talking on his phone—distracted. Rookie move number two.

Jeong-Ja moved a little to the right for a better look. That was when she spotted a second individual, which gave her pause. *A team?* There could be others spread out across the roof. Her best bet was to flank those two from the other side of the AC unit. Just beyond that was the edge of the parapet.

She tiptoed, sidestepping to the left in the shadow of the

water tank. She reached the corner of the parapet, which gave her a view of the other side of the AC unit. With the constant hum, Jeong-Ja figured she could make her way there without being heard. Seconds later, she had her back up against the AC unit with a knife in each hand.

43

"Those bastards!" Travers shouted as he watched the men destroy his cameras. In a matter of seconds, he'd lost all visuals on the building. "Gil, ready the drone. I am not missing out on this. I will capture the end of Sei on video."

Rocha grabbed the control transmitter for the drone and fired it up. He had to be careful as UAVs, or uncrewed aerial vehicles were illegal to fly within the city. Distance wouldn't be a problem, though. Pegasus was equipped with Mavic Air 2 drones. The drone had a range of eleven miles or eighteen kilometers and could move at 40 miles per hour or roughly 64 kilometers per hour.

"How long to get that thing in position?" Travers barked.

"Ten minutes, max."

Rocha flew the drone up about half a mile, more than enough to clear any building in its path without being spotted. When he reached Doyers Street, he descended to about fifty feet above Sei's building. The hum of the blades would only be detectable from ten feet away.

There were enough city lights for the high-definition camera on the drone to produce clear video footage of the area and most of the rooftops from that height. The drone would have to come in closer for more detail.

"If you go lower, can someone on the roof see the drone?" Travers asked.

"There's a chance they might hear the hum, but locating it would be a different story. It's tiny. It'll be hard to see against the night sky, but not totally impossible."

"Go lower and switch on thermal vision," Travers said.

Rocha did as he was instructed, and the footage on the drone's monitor turned blue, with orange and red spots picking up heat. Billowing steam from vents on the rooftops made it hard to detect human heat signatures. Switching to thermal also eliminated the detail they had before. Rocha flew around the building for a better view.

"Stop! What is that?" Travers asked out loud. "That looks like someone."

Rocha moved the drone back and lower so that they weren't looking directly down but at a twenty-degree angle.

"Looks like three men," Rocha said. He switched back to standard optics, and they could easily make out the men now that they knew where they were.

"We got here just in time for the show. Are you watching, Willie?" Travers asked.

"I don't see anyone else on the roof, just those three people," Rocha said.

"What are they waiting for?"

Rocha switched back to thermal optics.

"Look, there's another person just on the other side of the AC unit," Rocha said.

"Is that Sei sneaking up on them?" Travers said. "Wait, are we recording right now? We better be."

"We're recording. If you want, we can go live."

"Do that. Broadcast the feed to the same message room that the casino footage had been shown in. This will be wonderful."

Rocha switched back to standard optics, and fiddled with the ISO, the camera's sensitivity for light, for a clearer view. He started the live broadcast.

JEONG-JA HAD PEEKED around the AC unit and spotted the third man. They all seemed to be waiting. *Are there other men on the way?* It made no sense to her to come separately. *Maybe they're waiting for instructions? That seems more likely. They could have a visual inside the building. It's possible the building has already been breached, and these three men are covering the roof in case Sei uses it as an escape route. They have handguns, but that's it.*

Bored with waiting and theorizing, Jeong-Ja slipped around the AC unit and came up behind the last man. With knives in both hands, she punctured both sides of his neck.

Shunk!

Shunk!

She moved on to man number two before he could turn around. Jeong-Ja shoved one of the knives into his neck while she threw the other at the last man. It sunk into his left eye. Jeong-Ja finished off the man she had stabbed once with a clean cut across his neck and then silenced the other man quickly with the same slicing move.

The last man had made enough noise that if there were others on the roof, they'd come and inquire. Jeong-Ja quickly ducked back behind the AC unit just as something whizzed right past her face.

Joj-dwaesseo! There's a sniper!

No sooner had Jeong-Ja had that thought than she heard

another shot. But this one had come from a different shooter—the shot was muffled.

Two shooters?

A hand cupped around Jeong-Ja's mouth a few moments later.

44

"What the hell just happened?" Travers blurted out.

"That wasn't Sei that attacked those men," Gary said.

"Who would attack those men if not her?"

Everyone in Pegasus had just watched a young woman take out three grown men and escape nearly having her head blown off.

"Gil, find out who that person is. She has to be registered to even be at this location."

Rocha pulled up the register on his laptop. "Based on that outfit, I think I have an idea who it might be." He scrolled for a moment. "Got it! Her name is Jeong-Ja. She's from South Korea. She must dig cosplay."

"What the hell is cosplay?" Travers asked.

"It's when people dress up as their favorite characters from movies or anime cartoons or even video games. It's actually a huge deal. They have conventions all over the world and some of the top actors—"

"Can it. I didn't ask for the Wikipedia explanation."

Gary leaned in closer to the monitor. "Play that footage back again. Look right here." He pointed. "Just as Jeong-Ja ducks behind the AC unit, someone shot at her."

"Could that have been Sei?" Rocha asked.

"Well, from the angle of the bullet hitting that unit, it had to have come from across the street. Maybe she's camped out in another building."

"Gil, get that drone down there. I don't give a shit if people see it."

Rocha maneuvered the drone right down to the rooftops across the street and flew around. "If Sei was here, she's gone now."

"Pan across the windows of the top floor," Travers ordered.

The drone flew horizontally past the windows until it reached the tallest building.

"Move up to the top floor. Right there. Stop! That window's broken. Can you make the drone fly inside?"

Rocha maneuvered the drone carefully through a hole in the window the size of a basketball. The drone hovered near the window, and Rocha switched on the headlights so they could see inside the darkroom. A long table appeared with a man lying on top of it. Part of his head was missing and in his grip was a sniper rifle.

"Who is that?" Travers asked.

Rocha maneuvered the drone so they could see the man's face. "I don't recognize him, but I'll double-check the register. He could be a scavie."

"So it looks like this guy shot at Jeong-Ja," Gary said, "and someone else took a shot at him. I'm guessing it was Sei. Jeong-Ja drew the sniper out, and Sei took advantage of the opportunity."

"He's probably connected to the men Jeong-Ja killed," Rocha said. "And that's why he tried to kill her."

"Is it coincidence, or is Jeong-Ja working for Sei?" Travers asked.

"That's a good question," Gary said. "She very well could be."

"Gil, get that drone over to that AC unit, pronto!" Travers said. "And switch that goddamn live feed off."

KAZMER AND RADFORD were sitting in an SUV parked not far from the motor home. They'd been able to track down Pegasus earlier in the day, and Radford snuck up on it and placed a tracking device in the wheel well. They'd been following Travers ever since.

The two men were watching the live feed from the rooftop on a tablet that Radford held. "Travers was doing a great job up until just now. Now it looks like he has assassins killing each other. Not the best message to be sending out."

Just then, the video went dark.

"He killed the feed," Kazmer said. "I was wondering when that would happen."

"You know, I sort of feel bad for the guy. He's got an impossible job managing this contract while at the same time trying to save his position in the organization. I wonder if Ethan has been watching this."

"Probably not, unless he's got someone else managing us."

Radford flipped the tablet cover shut. "I wouldn't put that past him." Radford drew a deep breath and then let it out. "It's kind of a dick move, but I bet with all that's happening, you and I could probably head over to Chinatown and take Sei out ourselves. It would totally screw over Travers."

"You think it'll be that easy?"

Radford shrugged. "So far, I haven't been all that impressed by the talent that's come after her, so maybe she looks better than she really is."

Kazmer looked over at Radford. "You know what got Travers into his situation, right? Underestimating Sei. If you need a reminder, remember what she did to rescue her daughter."

"So what do you want to do? Just sit on the motor home?"

"We were told to keep an eye on Travers, not take over the contract."

"I guess I'm just curious. I mean, there has to be a reasonable explanation why assassins would be killing other assassins. Before you tell me they're fighting over the bounty, I'll counter by saying that's not what this looks like."

"I'll tell you what it looks like. It looks like Sei is winning."

45

I was a second away from ending the young woman's life when she uttered my name. And it wasn't just saying the word that gave me pause. Clearly she knew who I was, but it was the way her eyes lit up when she said it. It reminded me of someone: my daughter.

Against my own best judgment, I didn't follow through with killing her. Instead, I asked her a question.

"How well do you know me?"

"I've known you for years. I mean, not in the literal sense, but I've known of you since I first heard of you when I was younger."

"You're young now."

"I was eight when I discovered you."

I searched her body and found the thigh holster containing a small handgun. I took it out and threw it off the roof, along with a throwing knife she had tucked into a sheath on her other thigh. I also looked through her backpack and found additional throwing knives and a cell phone. I tossed those off the roof as well. The remaining items were of a personal nature: makeup, hairbrush, a small bottle of perfume, a pack of gum, hair ties, tampons, and a brochure for a convention in town. Not once did she try to stop me or fight back. It was bizarre for a so-called assassin.

"When people lie to me, one of two things happens," I said. "They die quickly. Or they die slowly."

"I swear I'm not lying. I used to be into hacking and spent a lot of time on the dark web. I stumbled onto these message boards for assassins and saw your strikes. I thought you were so awesome, so I started looking for any information I could find on you, which wasn't much. Mostly just your old posts."

There was a message board for assassins that I used to be active on when I was working. It's now defunct. I would occasionally post about my strikes. Strikes were successful kills. Assassins or mercenaries or whoever would post the information about their targets and how they creatively executed the kills. There was some truth in what she'd said.

"Continue," I said.

"The more I read, the more intrigued I became. I decided I didn't want to be an international hacker. I wanted to be like you."

"So you took a few night courses at the local assassin school near your home?" I looked at the knife I still had pressed against her neck. "You might want to ask for a refund."

She eyed the sniper rifle I had strapped across my back. "You have a suppressor on the rifle. You were the second shooter. Did you kill the other sniper?"

"You're lucky he was a scavie, or else your brains would be all over the place."

"So the men I executed were scavies as well. Hmmm, looks like I did you a favor."

"You're still alive. Favor returned."

I glanced around. It wasn't safe to remain on the roof. I promptly dragged her back to the bulkhead. I then marched her down the stairs and into the same room I had Tran kept in.

"Behave yourselves."

I left, locking the door behind me.

TRAN LOOKED the girl up and down. "Why you dress up for Halloween?" he asked with a big smirk on his face.

"It's cosplay, dumbass," Jeong-Ja sneered. "New York Comic Con is happening right now. Why are you here?"

"I'm a badass hacker. None of this make-believe shit."

"Oh yeah? Did someone hack into your face?"

"I'm working for Sei."

"Is that so?"

"You don't believe?"

"She doesn't need your help. She's more than capable."

"How do you know what she need and don't need?"

"I just know. You'll have to take my word for it."

Jeong-Ja took a seat at the computer next to Tran.

"You working on something for her?" Tran asked.

"I'm not sure yet. I think I was just hired."

"Why would she hire a girl who dress like a cartoon character?"

Jeong-Ja leaned forward and stabbed Tran in his bony chest with her forefinger. "Because I'm a badass assassin."

Tran let out a loud laugh. "If that's true, why did she lock you up in here with me?"

"Are you deaf? I just said she hired me."

"Where are your weapons?"

"She has them."

"*Do-hoi*. You crazy. You a prisoner just like me."

"Prisoner? I thought you said you were working for her?" Jeong-Ja mimicked Tran's nasally tone.

"I am. We have a deal. I help her, and she help me get out of here."

Tran told Jeong-Ja all about his involvement with Travers and helping him manage the contract.

Jeong-Ja raised an eyebrow. "*Sshi-bal*. Are you telling the truth?"

"Yeah, I not bullshit you. They bring me from Vietnam, and I been riding around in Pegasus."

"Pegasus?"

"This is the name of the motor home."

"So you update the dossier and stuff?"

"Yeah."

"How many assassins are on the contract?"

"A lot, but not everyone is chasing her now. A lot of people are outside America. You Korean, right?"

"Yeah, why?"

"You the first person I know that come for her from outside America. But it looks like you fail."

"I was here for Comic Con, really, and if the opportunity came up, I would try. Fifty million dollars is a lot. Are they really paying it?"

"Yeah. It's real. It's not bullshit."

Jeong-Ja leaned back in her chair. "*Daebak*. What I could do with that much money." She sat up quickly. "Do they pay you a lot?"

"Pay okay. I mostly come because I think it's fun and I want to go outside Vietnam. But now, they leave me to die. *Dit me may*."

Jeong-Ja laughed.

"You understand Vietnamese?"

"I know the swear words. Hey, can you show me the register? I'm dying to know who signed up."

"Yeah, no problem."

Tran tapped on the keyboard, and an animated briefcase loaded on the screen and opened up. Inside were animated pieces of paper. Tran clicked on the pile, and a piece of paper filled the screen. It had a picture of an assassin with their name and what country they were in or from.

"No way, I know who that is," Jeong-Ja said as she moved her chair right up against Tran's. On the screen was a Japanese woman dressed in a traditional red and white geisha outfit.

"That's Akako Sakamoto, the feared geisha assassin. Everyone calls her Red, though. I'm guessing because of the red she wears. She's one of my heroes."

"Is she good?"

"She's deadly. She kills with ordinary objects, like a fan or chopsticks, or even the pins that hold her hair up in a bun. Go to the next person."

Tran clicked on the arrow button, and a new profile appeared. This one had multiple pictures, all men, all holding large battle axes and swords.

"No way! That's that assassin family from Norway. Viking lineage, from what I heard."

"Vikings?"

"Yeah, the old one is the dad. The younger ones are his sons. I've never actually seen a photo of them. Just read some descriptions. But I heard they are brutal. They're known for splitting their targets in half. You don't want them hunting you."

"Do they have a nickname, too?"

"The father is called Olaf the Splitter. The rest are called whatever their name plus Son of Olaf the Splitter, you know because they split people in half."

"So this guy is Thord, Son of Olaf the Splitter."

"Yes."

Jeong Ja reached around Tran and took over fast-forwarding through the profiles.

"Esmeralda the Witch Doctor, Dorothy Crow, the Cork Brothers, Mr. Venice Beach, Oladele the Greedy. Oh my God! There are so many good assassins signed up. I never had a chance."

"You know all these people?"

"Not personally."

The following profile was grayed out.

"What happened here?" Jeong-Ja asked.

"This assassin, Iron Wolf, is dead. You didn't see the livestream?"

Jeong-Ja shook her head.

"She fought Sei in a casino. She was really good, but Sei cracked her head open with an ax. Now her profile is turned off."

"Wow, it never occurred to me that Sei had already eliminated people. Where's my profile?"

Tran typed Jeong-Ja's name into the search field, and her profile had a yellow tint on it.

"Why does it have that color?" she asked.

"It means you were possibly compromised."

"Possibly?"

"Yeah, you not dead. You can still attack her."

"Oh, I see. So what does she have you working on?" Jeong-Ja asked, wanting to change the subject.

"She wants me to find Pegasus. My old boss kidnap her friend, and she need to rescue him."

"I used to hack. Maybe I can help you."

"Okay, use that computer."

Jeong-Ja spun her chair around and fired up the computer. "What do you think she'll do with us?"

"I don't know about you, but she's letting me go."

"How do you know she's telling the truth?"

Tran stopped typing on the keyboard and looked at Jeong-Ja. "I don't know, but I don't have a choice."

46

I doubled checked all the doors, and none of them appeared to have any breach attempts. I was on the second floor, peeking through the curtains. The street below was quiet and empty. Most of the lights glowing in the apartment windows across the way had been shut off. I checked the dossier to see if there were any additional updates. There weren't, but a link to footage of what had taken place earlier on the roof was available. Travers had livestreamed the entire event. I could expect he would continue. He wanted everyone to see what he thought would be an easy elimination. Yet another dumb move. All it did was anger me.

I returned to my bedroom on the third floor to recheck my weapons and take stock of my ammunition. I was well prepared and had enough to stand my ground. I wouldn't be able to do it forever, but I didn't need to. We were in the middle of New York City. A shoot-out would draw NYPD to Chinatown very quickly. Hunkering down wasn't the plan. I had to get out of Chinatown, but to where? I wasn't quite sure yet. I figured Travers was still in the city. The footage captured earlier came from a drone, most likely piloted by him.

I was about to check on Tran and his progress when I decided to peek outside once more. To my surprise, the street below was no longer empty.

Standing in a row across the street were five men wearing long black coats and fedoras. I recognized them. It was Go Hiro —a group of five assassins from Japan, all brothers, all with the same name: Hiro. "Go" was Japanese for the number five.

I made my way to the second floor and readied my sniper rifle as I went. These men were extremely dangerous, and if I could eliminate one or two of them at that moment, I'd gain an advantage. I headed to a window that had ordinary glass, ready to make heads explode, but they had disappeared. I looked up and down the street, but they were nowhere. I pulled out my phone. None of the sensors on the roof or the entranceways had been tripped. I switched to the cameras on the building across the street. The lights to the dim sum restaurant were still on, but the place had emptied out, probably because of the gunshot earlier. The front door to the restaurant had been left open. Go Hiro had to have gone inside.

I headed to the secret stairway that led to the restaurant. Along the way, I traded the sniper rifle for the Rattler compact assault rifle. At the top of the secret stairs, I took aim at the door. It was then I wished Sanka had outfitted the kitchen with cameras. He did mention he had a couple in the walkway behind the building. I pulled out my phone and cycled through the different security cameras until I landed on the ones in the walkway. Then area was clear. Go Hiro had to be inside the restaurant strategizing. Could they enter Willie's place through the AC vents in the restaurant? I made my way to the door and pressed an ear against it. All I could hear was a soft hum. I cycled through the cameras outside the building. Doyers Street and the rooftop were quiet.

It wasn't my style to sit and wait. I had just as much of an advantage as Go Hiro. They didn't know where in the building I was or if I was even inside. The drone footage didn't capture me on the roof.

I pressed my ear back against the door, and that time I heard voices. They were in the kitchen. A beat later the door jiggered, and I pulled the trigger, emptying the entire magazine.

The steady stream of bullets had blown a large hole in the wooden door. Lying on the floor was one Go Hiro. *Four left.* I reloaded, shoved the muzzle through the opening, and opened fire, just missing another Go Hiro. He had dived for cover behind a stainless-steel storage cabinet.

Remaining in the doorway was a sure way to be pinned down and pumped full of bullets. I moved quickly into the kitchen and ducked behind a stainless-steel cabinet. Bullets pinged the cabinet and chipped away at the brick wall behind me. I pressed my face flat against the floor and spotted the shoes of one of the Go Hiro's. I took aim and popped off a few rounds.

Arrrgghh! a man yelled.

Bullets rained down on my position, destroying the shelving full of dry and wet goods near me. Bags of flour and jugs of cooking oil exploded. I reloaded and continued popping up and firing on my targets. The Rattler was deadly in close-quarters combat, but it also ate through bullets quicker than I would have liked. I popped out my magazine—it was half full. I had another magazine left on my utility belt. I wasn't sure how well armed Go Hiro was, but their ammo was on the decline as well.

I put my shoulder into the cabinet and pushed forward, using it as a shield wall. The cabinet skidded across the floor, slamming into a table. Still, I continued pushing forward while taking potshots in the general direction where I thought the remaining Go Hiro were taking cover. I slammed into something solid that stopped me dead in my tracks.

There was a pool of blood on the floor, presumably from the

one I shot in the foot. One injured. Three healthy. I popped up and fired until the magazine was empty. I sat back down and reloaded my last magazine before peeking around the storage cabinet. I didn't see anyone, and it was quiet. Go Hiro had fled the kitchen. It was only a matter of time before the police arrived.

I scurried over to the double swinging doors that led into the dining area. Each door had a round window. With my back against the wall, I could see one side of the dining room through the window. It was clear. Did Go Hiro flee the restaurant?

"Sei! Give up. You can't win." The gruff voice had a Japanese accent.

I never understood why people say to give up. Who in their right mind, in a situation like mine, would simply give up? It's not like they were there to escort me out of the restaurant. They might as well have said, "Sei, come out so we can shoot you with no effort involved."

Before another thought could enter my brain, bullets punched through the drywall I had leaned up against. I dropped to the floor just in time to avoid being sheared in half by their gunfire. I rolled over to the doors, stuck my muzzle out, and fired, backing them off so I could slip into the main dining room. I made my way over to a round table and flipped it to its side for cover. I continued to trade shots with Go Hiro. From my estimate, they were all on the right side of the restaurant, but spread out.

I could remain behind the table, empty the rest of my magazine, and not make a difference, but that wasn't me. Plus, we were on the clock; I heard sirens in the distance.

I took aim through the iron sights of my Rattler and moved forward, taking the forehead off the nearest Go Hiro. I tossed the empty assault rifle to the side and cartwheeled out of the other Go Hiro's line of fire.

I settled behind another overturned table. I still had both handguns, but only two Go Hiro left, and I knew exactly where they were. I decided to save the ammo and use my throwing knives.

Just as I was about to move out from behind the table, a buzzing noise caught my attention. I looked up and saw a drone pass overhead. *Travers!* He was watching and probably streaming the fight. Ethan could be watching. *If it's a show they want, a show they'll get. This is what happens when you come after me, Ethan.*

I shot out from my cover to the table where I knew a Go Hiro had taken cover. As I ran to it, the other Go Hiro opened fire. I had enough speed that I dropped to the floor and slid feet first toward an overturned table.

As I neared it, I readied my knives.

Ten feet away, the tip of a muzzle inched out from behind the table.

A second later, the tip of the brim showed.

Five feet away, I pulled a leg back but kept the other one straight.

Three feet away, the muzzle turned toward me.

I began my kick, and my boot caught the tip of the muzzle, knocking it up as it fired.

As I slid past the table, my eyes locked with the eyes of the Go Hiro who was behind it. I jammed my knife into his neck toward the rear so that it lodged in his spine. That's how I braked. I then punctured the other side of his neck repeatedly until he was motionless. *One more left.*

"You're out of ammo," I called out as I stood up. "And your brothers are dead."

From behind another table, the last Go Hiro stood. He still had his fedora on. He brandished two tantos, essentially

Japanese katanas but compact. The blades were only twelve inches.

He moved away to the other side of the table as he swung the tantos around in his hands.

"You will pay dearly for what you have done," he said in a gruff voice before charging at me.

I immediately threw both knives at him, but he deflected them with his tantos. He was upon me before I could pull more knives out of my utility belt. I side-stepped out of the way of a downward slash and then avoided the stab by the other tanto. I dropped low and swept him off his feet, but he bounced back to his feet quickly. It was enough time for me to arm myself with two throwing knives and cross them in an X for a static block. I yanked back, dislodging one of the tantos from his grip, and sent it clanking across the floor.

With lightning speed, his fist struck me square in my chest, hard, backing me away. He continued his advance with multiple slashes, which I deflected with my knives, but he was strong, and my last deflection caused me to lose one of my knives.

I threw my last knife at his face, but he was quicker, deflecting it with the tanto's blade before launching an all-out assault. I armed myself with my two remaining knives and barely escaped being beheaded in the process. I leaped over to a nearby table to put an obstacle between us.

He kicked the table up and over, sending the dishes on top of it flying my way. A teapot and a couple of teacups landed near my foot, and I kicked the pot, sending it straight at his face. He missed it with his tanto, and it slammed into his forehead, stunning him. He fought to regain his balance as he took a few steps backward. I kicked the remaining teacups and they rocketed toward him like cannonballs before I exploded, lunging toward his stomach and slicing his belly horizontally. I delivered a snapping kick to the side of his head. He wobbled, and I sliced his chest twice. None of the wounds were deadly. I needed to hit him in a vulnerable location.

Another snapping high kick; this one caught him on the chin and spun him around. I jumped onto his back, hooked my legs around his torso, and impaled his neck with my knives. I dropped off of him and watched him take a few wobbly steps forward.

Let me help you.

A swift kick to his back sent him flying forward into the support column in the restaurant. He fell to the floor. I picked up the tanto and drove it deep into his back until the tip clinked as it dinged the floor under him.

I looked back over my shoulder. The drone was still in the restaurant, hovering not far from me. I used my foot to kick a nearby teacup up into the air. I snatched it and then pitched it at the drone, but it deftly avoided being hit.

The sirens were close. I didn't have time to deal with the drone. I ran back into the kitchen and through the door I had destroyed earlier. Up the stairs I went to the room where I had Tran and the girl locked away. I needed Tran, but I didn't need her.

I kicked the door open. Both of them jumped in their seats before looking back at me. "You." I pointed at Tran. "Come with me. Now!"

"What about me?" the girl asked.

"Be thankful I'm not killing you. I usually do that when someone makes an attempt on my life."

"Wait, she's cool," Tran blurted out. "She's a pretty good hacker. Let's take her."

"New deal. If she makes one mistake, our agreement is off. Is that clear?"

"Uh, um..."

"I promise I won't try anything," the girl said. "I'm sorry for taking the contract. I was just stupid. I can help, though. I want to."

I walked up to her, grabbed her by the neck, and looked into her eyes. "Do not disappoint me."

I released her, and the three of us hurried to the restaurant kitchen and out the back door.

"This way," I said.

I led the way down the narrow walkway while staring at my cell phone. Before Sanka had left, he'd let me know about one additional enhancement made to the building—a fail-safe option. He had planted enough C-4 in the building to create a big enough explosion to eliminate all traces of anyone inside. The last thing he wanted was his DNA or that of his men being discovered. I certainly wasn't worried about my DNA. No database in the world could identify me. I thought twice about initiating the fail-safe. That was Willie's home I was about to destroy. Was there a chance we could come back from what had just happened, and he could return to life as usual? I highly doubted it. I pressed the button.

47

S hortly after hearing an explosion in the distance, the monitors inside Pegasus went dark.

"Sei must have set off a bomb," Gary said.

"We lost the drone," Rocha said.

"Get the other drone to that location!" Travers shouted.

Rocha launched the second drone and flew it to Chinatown as swiftly as possible. When the drone arrived at Doyers Street, it was apparent what had happened. All the windows and part of the building's brick structure had been blown out. A fire started spreading on the second and third floors as black smoke poured out of the windows.

Travers turned to Willie. "Do you see what your friend did? She destroyed your building. If I were you, I'd be so pissed off at Sei right now I'd want to see her dead. Is that a fair guess at how you're feeling inside?" Travers then moved closer to Willie and leaned in inches from the old man's face. "Sei ruined your life. She deserves to be punished, don't you think? Help us help you. Tell us what she's planning, and I'll make sure she gets what's coming to her."

"What about Duc?" Rocha asked.

Travers looked back over his shoulder. "What about him?"

"He's probably there."

"He's dead. You saw the building."

"But maybe he's not. Maybe he survived. Should we try to find out?"

"Hey, if you want to fly your drone into the building and poke around, go for it."

Rocha flew the drone through blown out window on the third floor. It was dark and smoky inside, so he switched on the headlights. The entire floor was in shambles, with destroyed furniture littering the place. The staircase had collapsed, so he couldn't fly the drone to the floor above, but a hole in the floor gave him access to the floor below.

"There's a room over there. Go inside," Gary said.

Rocha maneuvered the drone into the room, and they saw the remains of computers scattered across the floor.

"This is the room Duc was in," Gary said. "Look for a body."

The drone flew low to the ground, but they didn't see anyone or parts of anyone.

"You think he got out?" Rocha asked out loud.

Gary looked over at Travers. "You know, there is a chance Sei flipped him. We did leave him for dead, so there's a reason for a grudge. And if that's the case, he knows a lot about our operation here."

"Search the rest of the building," Travers said.

Rocha managed to fly the drone to the upper floors, but nowhere did they see any bodies.

"Unless he was locked away in a small closet or something, there's a chance he might have gotten out," Gary said.

Rocha flew the drone back out of the building. "I'll check the restaurant. We should try and confirm if Sei is dead or not."

The drone flew down to street level and into the restaurant. There was a lot of smoke and flames. They could see bodies lying on the ground, but none of them belonged to Sei. Rocha flew the drone into the kitchen, but the heat from the fire was starting to affect the drone.

"If I stay here longer, the drone will stop working. The plastic is probably already melting."

Rocha zipped the drone out of the restaurant and ascended.

"We have no proof Sei died in the explosion," Gary said. "We have to assume she got out before the explosion. And she might have Duc with her. Pegasus is in danger of being compromised."

"Gil, is it possible for Duc to hack into Pegasus?"

"Uh, yeah. He knows the system, but I can start putting things in place to counter that."

"Well, what are you waiting for? Start! And Gary, get us out of Lower Manhattan."

48

M y...I'll call them prisoners for now, and I exited the walkway behind the building onto Pell Street. From there, we headed west to Mott Street and then north to Bayard Street. I stuffed my two handguns into my backpack before hailing a taxi. Willie was the only solid connection I could trust in Manhattan, and now he had been kidnapped and his location compromised. But I still needed a place where I could formulate the next steps without looking over my shoulder, a place we could hide in plain sight amidst a sea of people.

The taxi stopped in front of the Marriot Marquis in Times Square. Even at eleven at night, the sidewalks were busy with tourists utterly unaware of what had happened in Lower Manhattan. I paid the taxi driver, and we headed inside the hotel.

"Don't talk to anyone. Don't look at anyone. Is that clear?" I asked.

Both Tran and the girl nodded. I still didn't know her name or care much, but I needed to call her something.

"What's your name?"

"My name is Jeong-Ja. I'm from South Korea. I originally

came to New York for Comic Con. It's the reason why I'm dressed this way, in case you're wondering."

I held up my hand. "That's enough for now."

I booked a suite for two days. If I needed longer than that to find Willie, I'd already lost. That and I really didn't feel like babysitting those two.

Once we were up in the suite, all Tran could talk about was going outside to look around and get something to eat. He said his last meal was at lunch. I wasn't sure when Jeong-Ja last ate. I ordered room service cheeseburgers and fries for them and a tuna fish sandwich for myself. The hotel had laptops they loaned out, and I'd requested a pair be delivered as quickly as possible.

"You two are not to leave this room. If you want to look at Times Square, the window is right there. Once you've finished eating, you will get to work. I need to find Willie."

There was a knock on the door. The laptops had arrived along with our food.

"Wow, I was expecting a piece of shit," Tran said as he picked up one of the laptops. "These are the new Macs. I can work with this."

"I'm starved," Jeong-Ja said as she grabbed a cheeseburger. "Thank you so much. I promise to pay you back one day."

"Do your job, and we'll call it even."

I picked up my sandwich and moved over to the sofa away from them. It didn't take long before Jeong-Ja sat next to me with her burger. Tran had sat himself down in front of the television and was watching a movie.

"Can I ask you something?" she said.

"No."

"Oh..."

As she ate her burger quietly, my curiosity about her grew.

"How long have you been an assassin?" I asked.

"Not long, really. I've never had a real contract, you know, one given to me where I got paid. I've only helped others on their jobs, but mostly I've just trained and—"

"Who trained you?" I asked.

"You probably don't know him."

"Try me."

"His name is Sung Ho. Have you heard of him?"

"I have."

"He's pretty good."

"No, he's not. I snuck up on you easily. You should be on the roof dead with those other men along with your short-lived career as an assassin."

"That may be so, but I do know how to handle myself. I have a good understanding of the basics, which I can continue to build on."

"Your understanding got you within an inch of death."

Jeong-Ja dropped her burger back on her plate. "Why don't you train me? I promise I'm a fast learner, and I'll be an excellent student. I've idolized you since I was a child. All I ever wanted was to be like you, and to be sitting right here, next to you, is beyond what I ever imagined. Please, please, please."

"No."

"Why not?"

"I'm busy."

"Okay, at least let me help you?"

"You are."

"No, I mean with your other problem, the contract. Duc said hundreds of assassins signed up to come after you. You need people you can trust to watch your back."

I raised a single eyebrow. "Excuse me, but if I recall correctly, you came after me. Why should I trust you? Why shouldn't I eliminate you right now? I already have Duc helping. I don't need two hackers."

"Because, if you wanted me dead, you wouldn't have hesitated back there on the roof. Admit it. You like me a little, right?"

I leaned back and ate my sandwich. I wasn't interested in debating with Jeong-Ja, but she did remind me a little of my daughter. Jeong-Ja had a similar haircut and energy, and that was probably it. Though, she was right: I should have automatically slit her neck without hesitation. And I had been seconds away, but as I came up behind her, her physique, the way she was crouched...it screamed Mui.

At that moment, I realized how much I missed my daughter. I know my personality. When I'm focused, I get into a mode where my emotions are nonexistent, but something was different this time around. I had lunch with a man I'd just met. I let a person who came after me live. Were these signs that I missed Mui? Never in my entire life had I ever made decisions like that. Well, there was a time, with Kostas. But it took years of patience on his end. He'd become very special in my life during a time when I was alone.

When Mui came into my life, I did notice small changes... normalization if I had to call it something. If people who knew me when I was younger could see me now, they'd say, "That's not the Sei I know."

Was that a bad thing? In the world of assassins, yes. But in the world I had created for Mui and myself, no. I had settled in nicely to my new life in Nafplio as a hotel owner. There, I was surrounded by people who cared about me but wanted nothing in return. There was warmth and love, something I'd only ever felt with Kostas. Having Mui back in my life changed things in ways that I could never have anticipated.

Unfortunately, my current situation was a stark reminder that I could never truly escape my past. It would always remain a step behind me, disrupting any chance of a normal life.

But what is normal?

49

W hile Tran and Jeong-Ja worked on finding a back door into Pegasus, I stepped into the bedroom and made a call to Jackson. All I had were two handguns and the extra magazine on my utility belt. I needed a resupply.

"I was expecting your call," Jackson said.

"And why is that?"

"The explosion in Chinatown made the news. I know Sanka well. I knew he would give you a fail-safe option. It must have gotten bad for you to use it."

"Willie was taken. I need to rescue him."

"You're adding to your to-do list, Sei."

"It's my fault. I have to take care of this."

"I understand. You're welcome to stop by anytime."

"I have a situation."

I quickly explained about the two prisoners I had acquired and why I couldn't leave them alone.

"So you want to bring them with you. That's not how I do business. You cannot vet them. This is my home. My family is here."

"I understand that. I'm asking for a favor."

"I'm sorry, Sei. You come alone, or you don't come at all. I can't do anything else for you."

I disconnected the call and walked out of the bedroom. "Have you found a way in?"

"I found Pegasus," Tran said.

"Where are they?"

"It's a place called Washington Heights. Do you know it?"

"I'm aware of it. It's in Upper Manhattan. Are they moving?"

"I don't think so. They're on 173rd Street, next to a park. Come take a look at the map."

I looked over Tran's shoulder. "That's a Dominican neighborhood."

"Yeah, so what? You think there are gangs there?"

"Trinitarios are a Dominican gang with ties to that area, but I can't be sure if they're operating there at the moment. Does the register log the location of participants?

Tran shook his head. "Just name, photo, and country so they can pay the right person, I guess."

Travers could have a connection to the Trinitarios and be using that area as a safe haven. I had to assume he thought I had Tran and was working with him for information. The last thing I wanted was to insert myself in the middle of a gang with numbers. I had enough headaches to deal with.

"Is there a way to kill the engine on that motor home?"

"Maybe. I still haven't found a back door into the mainframe, but don't worry. I'm still trying."

"Try harder. I want it immobile."

"What are you planning?" Jeong-Ja asked.

"Stand up and turn around." I removed a plastic cuff from my utility belt and secured Jeong-Ja's hands together.

"Duc, your turn."

"Wait, why are you putting me in handcuffs? How can I do my job?"

"I won't ask twice."

Tran got up, and I secured his hands behind his back. There was nothing for me to secure them to, but the chairs around the dining room table were large, heavy, and had metal legs. I handcuffed a chair to each of them. They would be mobile, but they'd have to drag a chair around.

"I'll be back as soon as possible."

"Wait, where are you going?" Jeong-Ja asked. "What do I do if I have to use the bathroom?"

I slipped my backpack on. "Hold it."

ABOUT AN HOUR LATER, my taxi stopped outside of Jackson's home. It was late, and most of the households in the neighborhood were asleep. I paid the driver and climbed out. Jackson, as usual, was waiting for me on his front porch.

"Sei, welcome."

"I apologize for my last-minute call and late arrival."

"It's okay. I understand. Come inside."

All of the lights in the lower level of his home were off except for the hallway light.

"My wife and kids are upstairs asleep," he said as I followed him down to the basement. "What are you planning this time, Sei?"

"I know where Willie is. He's in a mobile home. I need to conduct surveillance from afar."

"I have some excellent military-grade night vision binoculars."

"I need something mobile. What about a drone?"

A smile appeared on Jackson's face. "I like the way you're thinking, and I think I have the perfect one for you. Wait, do you know how to operate one?"

"I have someone who can."

"Okay."

Jackson disappeared into a small room for a few seconds and returned holding a large box. He quickly unpacked a drone that was much larger than the one Travers had.

"Do you have anything smaller?" I asked.

"Hear me out, Sei. It's very quiet. Allow me to demonstrate."

Right out of the box, Jackson could fire up the drone and have it hover in front of me.

"See how simple it is to get it flying? But the best part is that it can carry a fifteen-pound payload. Like explosives, for example."

Now I was the one who had cracked a smile. I hadn't planned to blow up the motor home because Willie was inside it, but getting rid of Pegasus would be ideal if I could get him out.

"I have a smaller one that's just as quiet with the same range, but it can't carry a payload."

"How would I set off an explosion with a drone?"

"You use an IED that can be set off by the impact. You need to be at least twenty feet above your target for it to work. Any lower, and it may not be enough force to set off the explosive."

"I take it you make these IEDs."

"For the drone, yes, but that's it. A contact taught me. I have the components, but they are unassembled at the moment. It's the only way Jalissa will allow me to keep it in the house. I can show you how to assemble it and attach it to the drone."

I'd worked with C-4 on numerous occasions, but what Jackson was talking about was something I'd never attempted. It sounded plausible. But I would also be relying on Tran to operate the drone and drop an IED on the motor home. I had no idea if he'd ever taken a life, let alone those of ones he knew.

There were a lot of open ends in the plan, which I wasn't a fan of.

"I need more ammunition and throwing knives."

"Done. Do you still have your assault rifle? What about the sniper?"

"Neither, but I don't foresee a need right now; just ammo for the handguns...and the drone."

"All right. Let me show you how to put the IED together."

———————

BY THE TIME I returned to the hotel, two and a half hours had passed. None of the hotel staff questioned me, carrying a box clearly marked on the outside with photos of a drone. If they only knew what else was inside the box.

I used the keycard to unlock the door to the suite and pushed my way inside. I set the box down, expecting a barrage of complaints about taking so long. There was a lot of shouting, but only from one of them. The other one was missing.

50

I drew my handgun out of my backpack and immediately searched the bedroom and bathroom.

"He's not here," Jeong-Ja shouted.

I walked out of the bedroom with my handgun pointed directly at Jeong-Ja. "Where is he?"

"He escaped."

I walked over to the chair Tran had been secured to. The plastic cuffs were still intact.

"How did he get out?"

"I'm not sure. I've just heard him grunting. And the next thing I knew, he slipped a hand free, probably because his wrists are so skinny. But you can't trust him, Sei. He's been playing you this whole time."

I placed my gun against Jeong-Ja's forehead. "How do I know you're not in on the plan?"

"I swear to God. I'm not," she said with a shaky voice. "He totally thinks you're dumb. He's still working for his boss. He left to meet them about thirty minutes ago. Free me, Sei. I can help." Jeong-Ja motioned to the laptop. "He did something on his laptop. Maybe he warned them. I can figure it out, but you have to free me."

I removed a knife from the utility belt and cut Jeong-Ja free, and she hurried over to Tran's laptop.

"Well?" I asked impatiently.

"I'm not sure. Wait, I have an idea." She tapped away at the laptop. "Oh, shit. I knew it. That little rat. The dossier is updated. It's saying the new location is here. It even has the suite number."

"We need to get out of here now!" I said.

"What about the laptops? Should I take one? I can still hack."

"Okay."

Jeong-Ja tucked the laptop into her backpack while I looked through the peephole. The hallway was clear.

"Follow me and do as I say," I said.

"Wait, the drone," Jeong-Ja said.

The last thing I wanted was to be bogged down with something while on the move.

"Have you flown one before?"

"Of course. Who hasn't?"

"Grab it."

Jeong-Ja picked up the box, and we left the suite, walking quickly to the elevators.

"Shouldn't we take the stairs?" she asked quietly.

"The elevator is faster."

I pointed my handgun at the doors just as the elevator doors opened. It was empty. We quickly made our way down to the lobby. It was half-past five in the morning. Tourists who had an early flight were checking out, and the early birds were starting their day.

"Where are we going?" Jeong-Ja asked.

"To Washington Heights. Do you know how to track Pegasus the way Tran did?"

"Yeah, I watched him while he did it."

"Okay, as soon as we're in the taxi, I want you to do that. They may not stay put long."

"I need internet access, but you threw my phone away."

"You can use my phone as a hotspot."

I had no idea if we were spotted on the way out of the hotel. I didn't think we were being tailed, but I couldn't be sure. I held my handgun against my lap pointed at the back of the driver's seat. At the moment, I trusted no one. Not even Jeong-Ja. I had let my guard down with Tran. I wouldn't make that mistake twice.

We got out of the taxi on 171st Street, two blocks away from J. Hood Wright Park, where Pegasus had been parked. Jeong-Ja had watched how Tran tracked the motor home and was able to do the same. Surprisingly, it hadn't moved.

"Something's not right," I said as we stood on the sidewalk.

The block was lined with residential apartment buildings six stories tall. Aside from a person walking their dog, it was quiet. But it wouldn't be long before the sun rose and people headed out to work.

I still didn't have a plan for Jeong-Ja. I didn't necessarily need her help, but she might come in handy. I wasn't quite ready to bomb Pegasus just yet. But I wanted a closer look. Jeong-Ja took the drone out of the box, along with the control box.

"What this?" she asked, pointing at a metal box that was also packed inside.

"Explosives. They attach to the bottom of the drone and can be dropped from above. The impact sets them off, but it has to be higher than twenty feet."

I wasn't sure if we needed the explosives, but I attached it to the drone anyway. A few minutes later, the drone rose quietly to the top of the buildings and then disappeared from sight. We focused on the monitor on the control device. The drone flew to 173rd, where Pegasus was parked.

"Go higher," I said.

Jeong-Ja maneuvered the drone upwards, and we now had a clear view of the entire park and the black motor home. The drone moved toward it and then circled above. From that height, we couldn't see inside. The interior lights also appeared to be off.

"Do you want me to go lower?" Jeong-Ja asked.

"Move the drone about six car lengths away from the front of the motorhome and then lower it to ten feet from the ground and zoom the camera in on the front window."

She did as I asked, but even with the high-definition video feed, we still couldn't see that clearly inside with the interior lights off. Either they were hiding in the back, or they had abandoned the motor home.

"You think they left?" Jeong-Ja asked.

"It's an expensive piece of equipment that's used to manage the contract. I doubt they abandoned it."

"Then they've set a trap. They want us to check it out."

I agreed with Jeong-Ja. Tran knew of my plans to rescue Willie, which meant Travers would now be aware of it if he hadn't already concluded I would do so.

"Duc has to be inside there," Jeong-Ja said. "He left long before we did. Do you want me to get closer? I can fly low to the ground, just inches above."

I nodded, and she flew the drone about a foot above the sidewalk until it reached a car parked in front of the motor home. The drone moved slowly forward until it was near the front right wheel.

"Loop around the motor home, but stay well below the windows."

Jeong-Ja did as I asked. She then moved along the bottom of the motor home, so we could look underneath it.

"I don't see any bombs," she said.

"Can you walk and fly at the same time?" I asked.

"Um, I'm not sure."

"Park the drone on top of the building across from the motor home. I want to get closer."

"Are you sure that's a good idea?" Jeong-Ja asked.

I looked back at her with a raised eyebrow.

"I'm just saying, it could be a trap. All you have is a handgun. I can't even provide backup because you threw mine away."

"Stay here and stay out of sight," I said.

"Well, at least let me provide coverage from above. I'll use the drone to keep watch over you."

I thought for a brief second about Jeong-Ja's proposal. It made sense. But she had also tried to come after me. I couldn't be sure that she'd given up that thought. I'd already ignored my usual way of dealing with threats, elimination. She should have never left that rooftop alive. And it didn't matter that I thought her skill level was probably subpar at best. It could be a clever ruse. Underestimating in my business can end up being a deadly mistake. But her innocence reminded me of Mui. I shook my head in disbelief at what was about to come out of my mouth.

"All right, but stay behind me and listen to everything I say without question."

Jeong-Ja was able to keep the drone flying above the motor home while we made our way to the park. We moved in toward the motor home, stopping near a tree beside the sidewalk. We were about fifty yards away.

"Stay here."

"Too bad you threw my phone away. I could have used it to alert you if I spot anything suspicious."

"Whistle. You *can* whistle, can't you?"

"Of course."

"Good. Earn your keep."

KAZMER AND RADFORD continued to shake their heads as they watched a replay of the drone footage capturing the fight in the restaurant and then the explosion.

"It's like a light was switched off," Radford said. "One minute Travers is killing it and doing a great job, and then this. Has he lost all sense of focus?"

"He's reaching for anything and everything without thinking things through," Kazmer said. "He's become more of a liability."

The two men were sitting in their car on the other side of the park from Pegasus.

"Maybe we should just go over there and have a talk with him," Radford said. "I feel like we owe him that. He's the one that vouched for us and brought us into the organization. If not for him, we wouldn't be working for Carmotte."

"I know, but we need to keep our distance."

"The guy is literally securing his place on the chopping block. Once Carmotte gets wind of what went down in China-town, he'll get rid of Travers."

Kazmer drew a deep breath and let it out. "He's been Ethan's loyal number two for a long time. It's hard to tell what's going through Carmotte's head."

Radford scratched at his chin. "I don't know. I just know that Carmotte can only blow things off so much, which he already has. Managing the contract was supposed to be Travers's comeback."

Kazmer shifted in his seat. "Look, the minute we knock on the door to that motor home, Travers is going to freak out. He'll know Carmotte sent us to be his eyes and ears. There's no getting around that. We need to keep reporting, and that means forwarding the latest footage to him. Keep thinking the way you're thinking, and you'll be the next one in Carmotte's line of sight."

"I get it. It just sucks watching the guy flounder around."

"What do you think will happen if we knock on that door? Are we going to relieve him of his duties? Three people making decisions will make it worse. He's been in worse situations. He might turn this around."

Radford undid his seatbelt.

"What are you doing?" Kazmer asked.

"I'm going in for a closer look. Don't worry. The sun isn't up yet. I'll use the trees in the park as cover."

51

Travers couldn't believe it when Tran contacted them. He thought the message Rocha received on the monitor wasn't from Tran, but Rocha believed it was because if anyone could hack into Pegasus, it was Tran.

Travers still wasn't entirely buying it. He asked Tran a series of questions that only someone who had been in Pegasus would know. And even then, Travers wavered, thinking Tran was answering the questions under duress. After twenty questions or so, Travers relaxed, and a plan was formed.

Was Tran bothered at all that they'd left him for dead inside the building? No. He knew from the beginning he would be on his own if things went sideways. But there was a huge incentive for him to come back into the fold. Tran's contract with Travers stated he would receive $5 million if the contract was completed. That was more money than Tran could ever imagine making on his own as a hacker. So Tran had remained patient and waited for the right moment. Jeong-Ja was the distraction he needed.

Inside Pegasus, Travers, Gary, Rocha, and Tran were sitting quietly in front of the monitors. Willie was sitting farther back and wasn't doing so well. The stress from the situation was beginning to take its toll on the old man. He moved in and out of consciousness and his breathing had become more labored.

Rocha took to operating his personal drone since the heat from the fire had damaged the other one. It was tiny, no bigger than the palm of his hand, and extremely quiet. It was equipped with high-definition, night-vision lenses that could also detect a heat signature. He had been flying it around the block while they waited for Sei.

Since no one inside Pegasus could handle Sei, Travers's best attack was to update the dossier with Pegasus' location. The downside was that they could get caught in the middle, especially if a lot of scavies showed up. However, the upside was that a large number of scavies would distract Sei and make her an easy target for a professional or even another scavie. All they had to do was sit back and watch the events unfold.

Rocha's drone picked up two heat signatures walking toward their location. He flew the drone above them and switched to standard optics. Everyone inside Pegasus recognized Sei, and Tran confirmed the other person was Jeong-Ja. It was Gary's eagle eye that picked up the other drone in the sky. It had flown near a streetlamp.

"Where is their drone going?" Travers asked. "Stay with it."

Rocha continued to monitor Sei and Jeong-Ja with his drone until they reached an area not far from the motor home.

"What are you doing there, Sei?" Travers thought out loud. "Are you formulating a plan? It won't work. We can see everything you're doing. Fly around the block. Let's see if anybody has shown up."

Rocha maneuvered his drone in a wide circle to cover the park, and the streets surrounding it.

"What is that?" Travers asked as he leaned in closer to the monitor. "Go back a little. There! Is that someone sneaking across the park?"

"It's a single person, so maybe a professional has arrived," Gary said.

Travers pumped his fist. "Yes! It's about to go down. Get it all on video. Don't miss anything."

Rocha flew the drone a little higher so that they could also see Sei. The unidentified person crouched behind a tree about twenty-five feet away from the edge of the park.

"He's waiting for Sei to make her move," Rocha said. "If he has a gun with great sights, he can pick her off easily from where he's at. But it doesn't look like he's carrying a rifle."

"Sei's on the move!" Gary said. "She's coming to us."

They watched as she moved closer to Pegasus. Travers could barely keep still as he watched with anticipation.

"Gil, move the drone up a little higher," Travers said. "I want a broader look in case others have shown up for the contract."

Rocha did as he was told.

"Higher. Don't worry; we can always swoop down quickly if need be. I want a bird's-eye view."

The drone continued to climb until the entire block and park were almost in view.

"Switch camera optics so we see heat signatures," Travers said.

The second Rocha did that, a collective gasp filled the room. Multiple heat signatures popped up all along the west side of the park, opposite Pegasus.

"Holy shit," Gary said. "There must be at least thirty people moving into the park."

"Scavies," Rocha said. "It has to be."

"It's the Trinitarios," Travers said. "They're a Dominican gang."

More heat signatures were picked up on the south side of the park.

"It has to be the entire gang with those numbers," Rocha said.

"No way Sei can take them all on and defend herself against the assassin hidden behind the tree," Gary said. "It's impossible."

Travers nodded. "This is a glorious start to the day. Yes, it is."

52

M y plan was to breach the motor home, eliminate the threats inside, and rescue Willie. And if I wanted this to happen before sunrise, there wasn't much time. I did a quick weapons check before making my final move to the motor home. A few seconds later, I had my back pressed up against the side of the motor home that faced the curb near the entrance.

"WHY DIDN'T HE SHOOT HER?" Rocha said quietly. "He missed a huge opportunity." Rocha lowered the drone. "Look! He's not even getting ready to attack. He's just watching."

"We could be wrong," Gary said. "Maybe it's not an assassin."

Rocha maneuvered the drone higher and to the West. "The Trinitarios are still advancing. They got the numbers to take Sei out." Rocha chuckled. "We all thought it would be some highly trained assassin that took the prize. Turns out, it could be a street gang that gets the glory and the cash."

"Gary, you locked the door, right?" Travers asked.

"Of course."

"Gil, get that drone back over to the motor home. I want to stay on Sei."

Rocha repositioned the drone over the Pegasus "Is she stabbing the tires? She is. She's letting the air out."

"Doesn't matter. The motor home can run on flats," Gary said.

"She's checking the door handle," Rocha said.

At that moment, everyone inside looked at the door. Willie began to move and call Sei's name.

"Tran, shut the old man up!" Travers said.

Tran punched Willie in the face. "Shut up," he said. "I will punch you again."

Travers raised his handgun and took aim at the door, but nothing happened.

"She's good," Gary said softly. "Checked the door without so much as making a single noise or movement."

According to the drone monitor, Sei was still outside the front door.

"What the hell is she doing?" Travers asked. "Gary, go check."

"Why should I check? The drone has eyes on her. We can see her perfectly fine on the monitor."

"The drone is too high to show us details."

Gary mumbled under his breath before grabbing a handgun and making his way to the front of the motor home. The windows were tinted, so it was too dark to see inside, except the front windshield. And even that one had a tint on the upper quarter part of it.

Gary stood near the two stairs leading down to the entrance door. If Sei was still outside the door, she was too close to the motor home for Gary to see her. He leaned forward, placing a hand against a wall to hold himself steady. He still couldn't see her. Gary looked back over his shoulder at Travers and shrugged. A popping sound rang out, and Gary collapsed to the floor.

"Holy shit. She shot Gary!" Rocha cried out. "Fuck! She's going to kill us."

Tran quickly armed himself with one of the compact assault rifles stored in the motor home.

"Hey, get me one too," Rocha shouted to Tran.

Travers kept his handgun trained on the front door. "Shut up! Do you want to alert the entire neighborhood that we're in here?"

"She just shot Gary. You think she doesn't know?" Rocha said.

"She still can't get in. Just stay the hell away from the windows. And don't forget, about forty gang members are converging on our location." Travers pointed at the monitor. "We just need to remain calm and let them do their thing."

I FIRED into the motor home, striking the man on the other side of the window. I wasn't able to identify him beforehand. But I was positive it wasn't Willie. *One down.*

Just before pulling the trigger, I heard Jeong-Ja whistle. Another whistle followed shortly after. This one was louder and with much more force. It prompted me to move to the motor home's rear, thinking Jeong-Ja spotted someone slipping out the back through a window. Not the case. All was quiet there. But inside the motor home, it was a different story. I'd recognized Tran's nasally voice. *That's right. Squirm, you little punk.*

RADFORD HEARD the shot and immediately drew his handgun. A second later, his phone buzzed. It was Kazmer calling.

"What happened?" Kazmer asked.

"Not sure. I'm still trying to work it out. Sei's out of my view at the moment. Wait... I just picked her up again. She's at the rear of Pegasus. She's armed."

"She shot into the motor home?"

"Your guess is as good as mine, but no return fire. What do you want to do? I mean, she's circling the motor home like a shark does its prey before it attacks. Hold on."

Movement to the right grabbed Radford's attention.

"I got multiple individuals converging on Pegasus' location. There must be at least thirty men. They look like they're armed with pointy machetes."

"Trinitarios. They're a Dominican gang. Back off and let them take over. It looks like Travers just got lucky."

"Roger that, I'm heading back to the car."

I HEARD MORE SHOUTING from Tran.

"No way! She told me if I double-cross her, she kill me. I'm not sitting here and waiting."

You're absolutely right about that.

"Shut up! Just shut the hell up!"

That's a voice I don't recognize. Is that Travers?

I was about to move away from the motor home's rear and back into the shadow along the right side when I noticed men had gathered at the edge of the park.

Scavies. This could disrupt my plan.

I needed to act quickly if I wanted to wrap up everything before sunrise. The men were gathering near the tree line at the edge of the park along the sidewalk. I didn't recognize them, but

I noticed the bush machetes they were holding. If I had to guess, they were Trinitarios. I held my position. One by one, they began to hesitantly exit the park onto the sidewalk.

Wait, Sei. Just a little bit longer.

More men emerged from the park. About twelve were cautiously moving forward.

Now!

I popped up and fired my first bullet in the forehead of the man furthest out front. Confusion on their part allowed me to quickly do the same to three others before shooting three more who attacked me. The rest had scattered for cover. I walked over to a parked car and fired at a Trinitario who had ducked down behind it.

"You bitch!" a voice called out from behind me.

A group of them were charging at me. I put two bullets directly in one man's chest. The lock on my handgun slid back, indicating I'd fired my last round.

I side-stepped and avoided the downward slash of a machete from a Trinitario before stepping into him and slamming my elbow into his mouth twice. I grabbed the machete handle and made him shove the blade down and into his stomach before avoiding a swiping machete from another Trinitario. It ended up in the face of the man I had just stabbed.

He dropped to the sidewalk as I delivered elbow strikes into the attacking Trinitario. I locked arms with the one holding the machete and spun him around, using his back to deflect another hacking machete. I kicked the screaming man in his stomach, sending him back into the Trinitario behind him.

I reloaded and fired at another attacking Trinitario, hitting him in his arm just as he wound up to slash at me. I pressed the barrel of my handgun under his jaw. I fired twice as I grabbed a throwing knife from my utility belt and threw it at another Trinitario, striking him in the neck. I moved in with a palm strike to the handle of the knife, forcing it further in before firing two rounds into his head.

This is taking too long.

I glanced back at the motor home, wondering if Travers had made an escape. Worse, was Willie dead? A second later, I was fending off another attack from the Trinitarios.

53

Jeong-Ja watched Sei on the drone's monitor from a comfortable distance away. She couldn't believe her eyes. Sei moved like a cat and struck precisely like a viper. She was better than Jeong-Ja could ever imagine she'd be. But from her vantage point above, she could see that Sei was seriously outnumbered.

This is my chance to prove to Sei that I can be trusted.

After landing the drone, Jeong-Ja ran toward the motor home. As she approached, the entrance door popped open and slid to the side. Tran jumped out with an assault rifle. He had the butt of the stock tucked into his shoulder as he peered through the sights, moving toward Sei's position.

Jeong-Ja had all her weapons taken except for two: a pair of mini push-daggers she kept hidden inside each of her ponytails. They were designed to look like decorative hairpieces. The blade of each was only about two inches long, but it was sharp and could inflict enough damage with multiple strikes.

It's payback time, you two-faced coward.

Tran had rounded the rear corner of the motor home, out of Jeong-Ja's view. She crept up to the rear of the motor home, prepared to strike the second she set eyes on him again. Tran was standing straight up and looking through the sights on his rifle. In the distance, she saw Sei fighting three men.

Jeong-Ja leaped forward. "Duc!"

Tran spun around just as Jeong-Ja punctured the sides of his neck. The rifle went off in the process, shooting rounds up into the sky. Jeong-Ja continued her attack, stabbing Tran as fast as she could, but he fought her off and backed away.

Bleeding profusely from his neck, he raised the rifle and pointed it at Jeong-Ja. "You stupid bitch. I should have killed you in the hotel."

Jeong-Ja threw one of the push daggers at Tran before diving behind a nearby car for cover. She knew she'd hit her target; Tran yelled out. Jeong-Ja scurried around the car to flank Tran and found him holding both hands up to his face. The dagger handle was sticking out of his left eye.

While he screamed in pain, Jeong-Ja rushed him and punctured his airway multiple times, causing Tran to choke for breath before she slashed his carotid artery.

Jeong-Ja grabbed the assault rifle and took aim at the men surrounding Sei. She had experience firing handguns but not a lot when it came to assault rifles.

You can do it. Just don't shoot Sei.

Jeong-Ja fired, and the kick was stronger than she'd anticipated. Her shot was high. She gripped the rifle tighter and lodged the butt into her shoulder.

Shoot the men away from Sei first.

She pulled the trigger and fired, hitting the man in his side. She pulled the trigger again and again, hitting the same man repeatedly in the torso until he dropped to a single knee.

Why won't you die?

She fired again, and this time the man fell to the asphalt.

FROM THE SIDE of my eye, I had caught a glimpse of Jeong-Ja firing in my direction. For a split section, I thought she had once again succumbed to the lure of the bounty. But when one of my attackers keeled over, I realized she was trying to help. And it looked like Tran was lying dead in the street.

I reloaded my last magazine. I had fifteen rounds and didn't want to waste them on the scavies. While they were easy to take down, they had the numbers to eat my remaining ammunition. I needed to save it for an assault on the motor home.

Jeong-Ja was busy fighting off two scavies. Figuring she could handle herself, I fought my way to the front of the motor home. There was a chance Tran had left the door unlocked when he came out.

Suddenly, rapid gunfire erupted from a shattered window on the motorhome. The bullets kicked up bits of asphalt all around me. A couple of scavies got hit. A cartwheel and two backflips put me behind the cover of a nearby vehicle. The shooter was in the driver's seat of the motor home. He wasn't targeting but simply spraying a wide area in an attempt to cover as much ground as possible.

I leaned out from the front of the car, took aim, and fired three times into the window. The gunfire stopped, and I ran straight toward the motor home. I crouched in front of it. Tran said there were four of them on Pegasus. I killed one earlier. Tran is dead. And whoever was shooting from the driver's seat was now dead. One left, plus Willie.

"Sei! You might have won that fight on the cargo ship, but I promise you won't win here."

Travers!

"Take one step into the motor home, and I will not hesitate to put a bullet into this old man's head."

A scavie ran up to me, and I fired two bullets into his chest. Another came from a different direction, and I fired once before he tumbled toward me. I fired another round into the top of his head and grabbed the machete from his hand.

I have to get into that motor home before I run out of bullets.

"There are too many of them, and more are on the way. Everyone knows your location. It's over, Sei."

I heard laughter inside the motor home. I imagined Travers had a gun pressed against Willie's head. They were toward the rear. The lights were off, affecting visibility. I had to breach the motor home in a way that I could fire the first shot accurately.

I wasted more bullets on two more scavies. By my count, I had five rounds left.

A gun fired inside the motor home, and Travers laughed.

"Did that bullet kill Willie?" he shouted.

Another gunshot rang out.

"Or did that one kill Willie? That's the question, Sei."

The scavies continued their attack. There were maybe ten of them circling around me. I could drop five of them and empty my magazine and still have at least five to deal with. Or I could resort to fighting them with the machete to save my bullets. But that would only eat up valuable time. Neither option was ideal.

Another gunshot from inside rang out.

"Time is running out, Sei!"

That gunshot was louder, and his voice sounded closer. Travers had moved to the front of the motor home, most likely using Willie as a shield.

Advantage: Me.

I'd have better visibility, but still only one shot.

JEONG-JA HAD CONTINUED to fire on the men, gaining the attention of two of them. With their machetes raised, they charged at
her. Jeong-Ja backed away while shooting, her shots missing her
angry targets. She struck one of the men in the chest at just five
feet out, and he fell to the road. But the other was upon her in
seconds, slashing down with his machete.

Jeong-Ja lifted her rifle up just in time to deflect a machete
strike. The man hacked at her repeatedly. Each blow loosened
her grip, and his attacks were still too quick for her to aim and
fire the rifle. It took all she had to stop the machete from splitting her face open. As she backed away, Jeong-Ja stumbled when
the heel of her shoe caught the curb. Her other foot followed,
and Jeong-Ja lost her balance, falling backward onto her butt,
hard.

A CRY for help caught my attention. I saw Jeong-Ja on her back
with a scavie attacking her with his machete. I had scavies
attacking and a madman holding Willie hostage. I needed
Willie's help to end the contract. Jeong-Ja was a liability.

I fended off more attacks using the machete and three more
bullets.

Two rounds left, Sei.

"Sei!" Jeong-Ja called out once more. "Please help me. He's
going to kill me!"

Another gunshot rang out from inside the motor home.

You need Willie, Sei. He can find Ethan.

I hacked the arm off a scavie and then shoved my machete
up into his jaw, lodging it in his skull. Another scavie appeared
on my flank. I had no choice but to fire, hitting him square in the
forehead.

One bullet, Sei.

"Help! I can't hold him off any longer! Sei, please!"

"Make a choice, Sei," Travers shouted.

He's looking outside!

I grabbed the machete from a dead scavie and shot out from the front of the motorhome while raising my firearm up. I ran in a slight arc, far enough away from the motor home to catch a glimpse of Travers through the front windshield. He held Willie in front of him.

"Sei!" Jeong-Ja screamed.

I fired and threw the machete.

The bullet punched a hole through the windshield.

The machete flew end over end toward the scavie.

Two strikes a second apart, and I couldn't yet tell if I had successfully hit my targets.

54

If you'd asked me twenty-four hours ago how I thought this night would have turned out, I would have given you the wrong answer.

What started off as a simple dinner with Willie had turned into kidnapping and having two people, whom I should have killed, do my bidding. I found myself having to choose between saving Willie, who could help me end the contract on my life, or save a wannabe assassin who accepted the contract to kill me.

Whether or not I could have stopped Willie's kidnapping was something I would always have play over in my head. As for Jeong-Ja, I don't have an explanation for trying to save her except that it's probably the same reason I didn't execute her back on the rooftop.

The machete struck the Trinitario in his torso, injuring him enough to give Jeong-Ja the upper hand. My help ended there. I turned my focus onto Willie. I disarmed another Trinitario and stabbed him in the belly before opening the door to the motor home. Surprisingly, it was unlocked.

The door popped out and slid open. I stayed off to the side in the event Travers was alive and armed. No shots were fired.

"Sei," a weak voice called out.

I went into the motor home and found Willie on the floor. A large knife was stuck in his chest. Travers lay dead next to him. My shot had struck him in the head.

"Willie, don't worry. I'll get you medical attention. Can you walk?" I asked as I tried to sit him up.

"Sei, stop. Listen to me. There's not much time." He said with labored breath.

"I know, Willie. I need to get you to a hospital. You're bleeding heavily."

"Sei, my time is here. But you must go on."

"Willie, you can't... Stay with me."

Willie could barely keep his eyes open, and his breaths were barely there. "There is one person who can help you."

"Who can help me? Who is better than you?"

"Kratica."

"Kratica? I don't know who that is. Where are they? How can I get in touch?"

Willie placed his hand on my arm and squeezed before taking his last breath.

"Willie?" I tried to wake him, but he was gone.

Footsteps behind me grabbed my attention. I looked over my shoulder and found a Trinitario ready to chop my head off. A beat later, the tip of a machete popped out of his stomach. His eyes bulged as he looked at the machete sticking out of his abdomen. The blade retracted, and blood gushed from the wound as he dropped to his knees. Behind him was Jeong-Ja holding a bloody machete.

"Sei! Come on. The police will be here soon." She held her hand out to me. "We have to leave now!" Jeong-Ja helped me to my feet and began pulling me out of the motor home.

I stopped and looked at Willie once more. My friend was dead. I had broken the promise I'd made to him, that I would protect him and let no harm come his way. I couldn't believe I'd failed him.

"Sei, you still have a contract you need to cancel. Don't let Willie's death be in vain."

She was right. I had to keep my chin up and continue pushing forward after Ethan. There wasn't a second-place winner in this game.

"Wait for me," Jeong-Ja said before running to retrieve the drone.

"We don't need it," I said when she returned.

"And we don't need Pegasus either."

As we hurried away from the motor home, Jeong-Ja maneuvered the drone above Pegasus. When it was high enough, she released the payload. The IED landed on the roof of the motor home triggering a large explosion. The windows blew out, and it caught fire. We continued to run as sirens could already be heard in the distance.

A block later, we hailed a taxi just as the sun had begun to crack the horizon. I wasn't sure of my next steps, so I told the taxi driver to head south. At the moment, I wanted distance between what was left of Pegasus and us.

QUINN STOOD in the shadows of a building across from the park. He had witnessed it all, everything from a woman single-handedly fighting an entire street gang to a motor home exploding. He couldn't believe the person striking men down like they were dominoes was the same petite woman he'd met at the gym and had lunch with earlier.

It would have made a lot of sense if a film crew was just off to the side, and he heard a director yell "Cut!" But that didn't happen. There were dead bodies strewn all across the road next to a motor home that had exploded and was now engulfed in flames. Quinn thought maybe if they were in some war-torn city, it would have some semblance of normalcy, but they were in the Big Apple, New York City.

Quinn had done his best to pick this woman's brain for information in the short time he'd spent with her. But she had remained tightlipped about any information about herself, even her name. But after watching her in action, he no longer had to wonder. There was no doubt in his mind that she was Sei, the woman he'd heard so much about.

55

Kazmer and Radford had wasted no time getting out of Washington Heights. After watching Pegasus explode, they realized Travers had lost the battle, as well as his life. There was no salvaging either one. A fast retreat out of New York City was in order.

After initiating the contract for Sei, Carmotte moved locations every two weeks—not at his own insistence, but at Travers's. The moves made Carmotte more ornery than usual. Kazmer and Radford were on the receiving end of his childish tirades since Travers was out managing the contract.

With Travers no longer there to steer a ship with a lunatic for a captain, both men wondered what would become of the Carmotte's organization. They didn't wait until their arrival at Carmotte's most recent hideout to deliver the news about Travers and the multimillion-dollar Pegasus. They placed a call as they raced away from the park.

"What do you mean he's been compromised?" Carmotte had shouted on the other end of the phone call. "How could Travers ever let it get this bad? Don't answer. I already know why. His downfall was underestimating Sei. Let this be a lesson to you two. And if I recall correctly, you two were supposed to prevent something as stupid as this from happening. Please don't tell me you're already becoming like Travers."

"It was unavoidable," Kazmer answered. "Travers used Pegasus as bait. It was a bet he had lost."

"Be that as it may, you should have figured out a way to stop it. What about Pegasus? Where is it now?"

"It's on fire."

"On fire? What happened?"

"We're not sure, but there was an explosion. Maybe Travers had a fail-safe built in. The good news is that any evidence of what was taking place inside it or what bodies it held will be destroyed. We're on our way back to you now."

"I hope you have solutions as to how the contract will be managed."

"We're working on a plan."

"Good, because you two will be managing the contract from now on. Oh, and one more thing, Kazmer. I need a number two. Don't disappoint me."

WHILE WE RODE in the taxi, Jeong-Ja and I sat quietly. I was thinking about the next steps. Willie had told me to find Kratica. Why hadn't Willie mentioned this person before? I had so many questions, with no clear direction on where to look for answers.

"What are we going to do now?" Jeong-Ja asked quietly.

"There is no 'we.' If I were you, I would find your friends and leave New York."

"But I don't have any friends here. The people I went to the convention with were people I had met online. I only met them for the first time when I came here."

"Then I suggest you book the next flight back to Korea."

"What about Kratica?"

"What do you know about Kratica?" I asked.

"Nothing. I just heard you say that name when you were talking to Willie. Is that someone who can help you?"

"I don't know. Willie said Kratica could help me."

"So you will look for Kratica?"

"You're a nosy little girl, aren't you?"

"Sorry, it's just that, well, I don't really have anything mean-ingful to go back to in Korea. I was sort of hoping that I could, you know, maybe help you—"

"No."

"Why not? I'm sure I can be of help. If it wasn't for me, you would be in the motor home lying next to Willie, your body burning in the fire," Jeong-Ja said as she lowered her voice.

"And you would not have been able to help me had I not saved you while you were pinned down on the sidewalk. We're even."

"Actually, if it weren't for me being in the hotel room with Tran, you wouldn't have known where he had gone. So we're not even."

"I didn't throw you off the building. We *are* even."

"I was the distraction you needed to spot that sniper in the building across the street."

"You were doing nothing more than eliminating what you thought was your competition on the contract. Let's not get ahead of ourselves here."

"I had a lot of opportunities to run, but I didn't, you know. I get it. You don't trust me, but I swear that's all behind me now. You need help finding this person if you're to cancel the contract. Come on, Sei. Everyone needs help. Sheesh."

Jeong-Ja had a background in hacking. Her offer to help me was tempting. Considering I had no info on Kratica, it might take both of our skills to find this person.

"There are rules," I said.

"Yes, of course." Jeong-Ja sat up straight. "I've followed every rule you've given so far. I can continue."

"I will add to the list of rules whenever I feel it's appropriate."

"As you must."

"No questioning my decisions."

"Your word is the law."

"I don't trust you yet."

"I'll work hard to earn your trust."

"This arrangement is temporary."

"I just want a chance to prove myself."

My gaze shifted to the passing scenery of New Yorkers filing out of their residences and starting their workday. I had successfully dismantled a piece of Ethan's inner circle, leaving a flank unguarded. While the effort had come with a significant loss, Willie, I had to continue. The game Ethan wanted to play was winner take all. There could be no other outcome.

"Please take us to JFK International Airport," I said to the driver.

"Are we flying somewhere?" Jeong-Ja asked.

"I have a friend I believe can provide us with a safe place to stay while we try to locate Kratica."

"Can you trust this person? The bounty on your head is huge, so, you know, a lot of people will turn on you."

"I believe I can trust him."

"I hope so. Where is he anyway?"

"Iceland."

CONTINUE THE SEI SERIES: If Plan A is your best shot at staying alive, Plan B is winging it. In the next installment, Sei's plan to

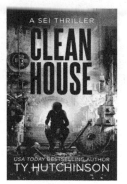

hunt down Ethan gets flipped on her when she discovers someone else is trying to break down her inner circle.

ALSO BY TY HUTCHINSON

Abby Kane FBI Thrillers

Corktown

Tenderloin

Russian Hill (CC Trilogy #1)

Lumpini Park (CC Trilogy #2)

Coit Tower (CC Trilogy #3)

Kowloon Bay

Suitcase Girl (SG Trilogy #1)

The Curator (SG Trilogy #2)

The Hatchery (SG Trilogy #3)

Find Yuri (Fury Trilogy #1)

Crooked City (Fury Trilogy #2)

Good Bad Psycho (Fury Trilogy #3)

The Puzzle Maker

The Muzzle Job

Abby Kane Thriller #15

Abby Kane Box Sets

Abby Kane Box Set 1 (Singles)

Abby Kane Box Set 2 (CC Trilogy)

Abby Kane Box Set 3 (SG Trilogy)

Abby Kane Box Set 4 (Fury Trilogy)

Sei Thrillers

Contract: Snatch

Contract: Sicko

Contract: Primo

Contract: Wolf Den

Contract: Endgame

Dumb Move

Clean House

Sei Box Sets

Sei Box Set 1 (1,2,3)

Mui Thrillers

A Book of Truths

A Book of Vengeance

A Book of Revelations

A Book of Villains

Mui Summer Thrillers

The Monastery

The Blood Grove

The Minotaur

Darby Stansfield Thrillers

The Accidental Criminal

(previously titled Chop Suey)

The Russian Problem

(previously titled Stroganov)

Holiday With A P.I.

(previously titled Loco Moco)

Darby Stansfield Box Set

Other Thrilling Reads

The Perfect Plan

The St. Petersburg Confession

Published by Ty Hutchinson

Copyright © 2021 by Ty Hutchinson

Cover Art: Damonza

38056787R00152